Written by Jamie Childress

Illustrated by Chris Braun

Galactic Treasure Hunt – Lost Fortress of Light

Written by Jamie Childress

Illustrated by Chris Braun

ISBN: 978-1-935487-06-7

Printed in the United States of America

First Printing September 2010

Printed by Color House Graphics Inc.

Grand Rapids, MI 49508

(Month and Year Files Submitted to Color House Graphics)

Published by

Adventures Unlimited Press

One Adventure Place

Kempton, Illinois 60946 USA

auphq@frontiernet.net

www.adventuresunlimitedpress.com

For: Cameron, Finn, Kira and Hatcher…

…for reminding us that every day can be an adventure.

Special thanks to Satchi Nita, Clay Dubofsky and the other friends and family who helped edit this book. Finaly, thanks to everyone who bought enough copies of our first four books to encourage us to try another.

About the Author – Jamie Childress:
When he's not writing stories, Jamie Childress is an aerospace engineer who works for Boeing's Research and Technology division. If he could find a wormhole, he would definitely want to visit another universe.

About the Illustrator – Chris Braun:
Chris works as a graphic illustrator for Boeing. When he's not doing that, he enjoys playing with his kids, karate, drawing and computer games.

Table of Contents

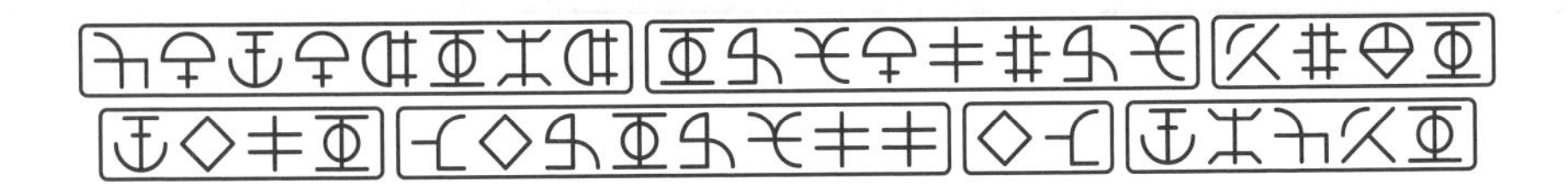

Prologue

It started out as a typical lazy summer. Jake and his brother Scott were enjoying their summer vacation. Fortunately for Jake and Scott, their do-nothing summer blasted off into adventure when a space alien named Nojo landed in the woods behind their house.

Nojo is a space archeologist from a planet in the constellation of Orion. He's searching for lost Delphian treasure. The Delphians are an alien race that vanished thousands of years ago. They left behind fantastic riches all over the galaxy. Nojo is searching for a great treasure called the Pillar of Knowledge which is the ancient computer library of the Delphians. It contains fabulous inventions and answers to the mysteries of the universe. When Jake and Scott first met Nojo, they accidentally touched a spherical key he had found. The computer codes in the key were transferred into Jake and Scott. Now

they are the "key keepers" and their heads hold the computer keys to unlock the waypoints to the Pillar of Knowledge. A waypoint is like a road sign along the path to the Delphian's long lost treasure. To find the treasure they have to find the next waypoint.

Nojo needs Jake and Scott to open the waypoints. So he takes them on his adventures to far away places. Their adventures have taken them to the moon, Atlantis, the days of the dinosaurs, the future and even to a lost universe. When they visited the lost universe, they made friends with King Bandilar and his daughter Kefreti on the planet Alsera. Read "Galactic Treasure Hunt #3- Lost Universe" to get the full story.

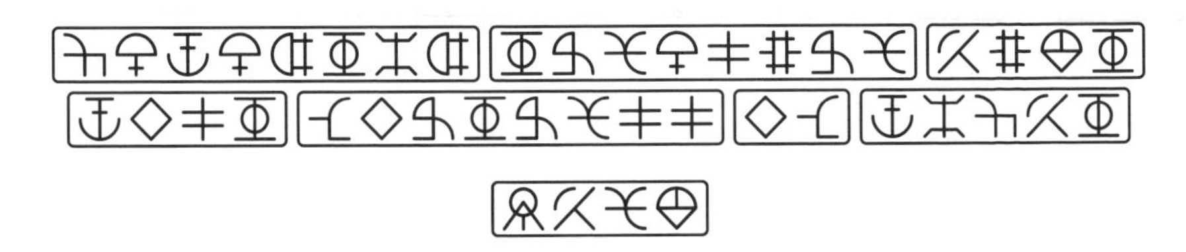

1 The Starship Arrives

Jake felt his half of the radio vibrate in his pocket and instantly stopped swinging his plastic light saber at his brother. Scott couldn't resist the easy opening in their light saber duel. He bopped Jake on the head lightly and said, "Score!"

Jake gave his brother a glare and shook his head. "No way! I'd already stopped," declared Jake as he pulled the piece of his radio from his pocket. "Nojo finally called us."

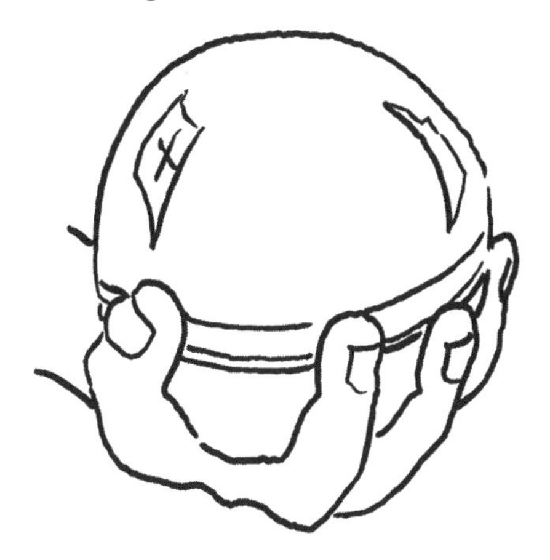

"I knew that. I was just messing with you," replied Scott, while dropping his light saber and handing his own piece of the radio to Jake for assembly. "It's about time Nojo called. It's been a week since we heard from him."

"Eight days actually," corrected Jake, as he twisted the two halves together and held up the completed radio. "He used to call us almost every day."

The little round radio made two short beeping sounds to indicate it was turned on and working. That was it, nothing else. The boys expected Nojo's cheerful British sounding voice to pop out of the radio. But, no, there was nothing.

This was so odd, that at first the boys just stood there waiting. Finally, Jake spoke up, "Hello, Nojo. Are you there?"

Scott looked at Jake and shrugged his shoulders. "Maybe it's broken," he suggested.

Jake thought for a moment then replied, “You might be right. Let’s go to the meadow. Maybe he’s there and we just can’t hear him.”

Scott went into the laundry room to tell his mom where they were going. “Mom, can we go play in the woods for a bit? We’re looking for our friend Nojo.”

Their mom stopped folding laundry for a second and replied, “Sure, honey. I hope you find him. You haven’t played spaceman in awhile. Just be back by 5:00. We’re having spaghetti for dinner.”

“We will,” promised Scott. Then he headed for the back door with Jake.

Jake took the radio apart and handed Scott his half when they got out side. “Let’s go,” said Jake simply.

The brothers started to trot down the well-worn trail to the meadow. As they went along, they ran faster and faster. These two rarely walked anywhere, but today it was a race to see Nojo.

“He’s here!” yelled Scott when they arrived at the meadow.

The starship was floating right in the middle of the meadow, just like every other time they’d met

Nojo here. The boarding ramp was down, but Nojo was not standing beside it.

The boys ran right up to the boarding ramp. "Hey, Nojo! Nojo!" they both called. But they didn't get an answer. No Nojo. No answering call from within the ship. Silence.

"This is weird," said Scott getting just a bit concerned. This, in itself, was odd since Scott almost never got concerned about anything.

"Very weird," agreed Jake. "Maybe he's hurt on the bridge deck or something. We need to check it out."

They trotted up the boarding ramp and hurried to the bridge deck. When they got there, it was empty. They called Nojo's name, but all they heard in response was the gentle whir of the boarding ramp closing behind them.

The next thing they knew the starship zipped out of the meadow in the blink of an eye. They were headed directly for the moon.

2 Autopilot

"Hey, who's driving this thing?" asked Scott.

"I don't know," replied Jake. "But we should take over before it crashes into something."

Both boys sat in their normal chairs on the bridge deck, and Scott announced, "I want to fly first. I never did get to fly low over the Moon. That looked fun."

"Okay. But we'll zip around the Moon later," said Jake. "First, we've got to find Nojo. Maybe he's back in the meadow."

Jake grabbed the control stick on his seat and tried to turn back towards Earth. The spaceship did not respond to his inputs. Scott tried wiggling his control stick too, but the ship kept heading straight for the Moon.

"Okay. Maybe Nojo's controls work," thought Jake out loud.

Jake got up from his own seat and sat at Nojo's control station. Nojo's control stick had no effect either. The ship entered the Moon's orbit and headed for the wormhole on the back side.

"None of the controls work. It must be on some kind of autopilot," concluded Jake.

"So let's turn it off," said Scott starting to poke at the alien symbols on Nojo's control pad.

"Stop!" Jake commanded frantically. "You don't know what those buttons do. We're about to enter the wormhole. If you touch the wrong one when we enter the wormhole, it could be worse than when we got lost in time. We might never get back."

Scott stopped. He realized his brother was right. "Sorry. I just hope we're being taken somewhere cool. Do you think there's a planet where candy grow on trees?" he asked jokingly.

A moment later the starship accelerated to light speed. The Moon and stars turned into blurs of rainbow light, and the wormhole began to wail. A strange sensation filled Jake and Scott's bodies. The atoms inside them shifted and vibrated like sand in a whirling bucket. If this had been the first time this had happened, they would have been frightened. But they both knew what this meant. They were being transported to another universe.

When they popped out the other side of the wormhole, both boys gazed at the planet growing larger in the viewing screen. It was a planet with blue water and soft inviting clouds. The only land was one large continent at the very top. Orbiting the planet were two small moons and one large moon. They recognized it instantly. It was Alsera.

"That explains it," announced Jake. "Nojo must want us on Alsera."

"But why didn't he call us?" quizzed Scott.

"I don't know," replied Jake. "Maybe the radio doesn't work between different universes."

"Then why didn't he come in the ship?" quizzed Scott again.

Jake thought about that one for a minute. "We haven't searched the whole ship," he replied. "Maybe he is here and we just haven't found him yet."

"Then let's start searching," said Scott. He immediately got up and headed over to a stairway at the back of the bridge deck. "I'll search the rooms at the top of the ship. You search the rooms in the bottom half."

"Good plan," agreed Jake. "We'll meet back here."

Nojo's ship was rather small for a starship. It was not much bigger than a large house. So it didn't take long to search.

Jake took the circular stairway down into the belly of the craft. The main room was where the electro-gravity capacitors were held. They glowed with a soft blue light and hummed quietly, all the while propelling the craft through space in a gravity bubble. Nojo was not there, nor was he in the other small rooms in the lower hull. These rooms held spare parts and banks of computers.

The upper rooms were all on the same level as the bridge deck. The first room that Scott found was

Nojo's bedroom. Scott didn't want to invade Nojo's private space, so he didn't go in. But from the entrance he could see Nojo's small bed, dresser, and desk. Nojo clearly wasn't in there. The only other room on the upper floor was a storage closet. When Scott opened it, he smiled and reached in for some things that he knew would be good to have on Alsera.

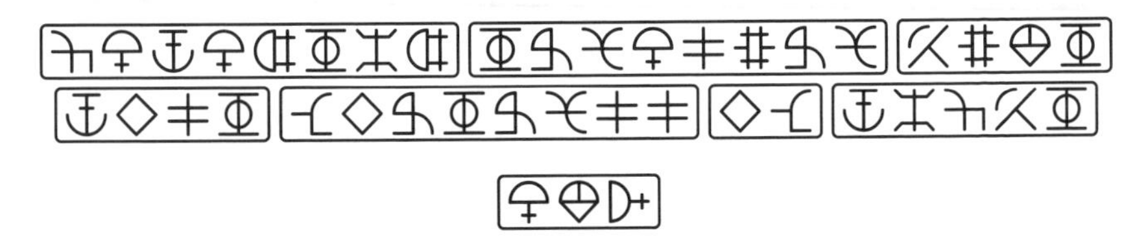

3 Alsera Again

When Jake climbed back up the stairs to the bridge deck, he found Scott standing next to a pile of gleaming silver metal, dull brown cloth, and sturdy brown leather. It was their ultanium swords, chain mail armor, translators, and old fashioned clothing from their last trip to Alsera.

"I didn't find Nojo, but I did find our gear from our last trip here," announced Scott with pleasure. "I'm glad we've been practicing our sword fighting."

"Yes, that might come in handy," agreed Jake. Then he looked out the forward viewing screen and saw that they were now hovering just outside King Bandilar's castle. "Let's put it on. I think we're about to land."

Scott got out of his normal clothes and got into his armor. As he buckled his sword scabbard to his belt, he asked Jake, "Do you think we'll still have super powers on Alsera?"

"I hope so," replied Jake as he got dressed himself. "I don't see why not. I expect that our atoms still vibrate at a different frequency than the atoms in this universe. So that will make us fast and allow us to move through walls. The gravity here would still be less than Earth. So we'll be strong."

At that moment the starship stopped just off the ground and the boarding ramp opened. They could hear excited barks, howls, and growling sounds outside the ship. That reminded Scott of the last piece of gear he needed to put on.

"Don't forget your translator," reminded Scott, as he picked up a large silver medallion at the end of a chain necklace.

"Yep, gonna need that for sure," replied Jake, picking up his own medallion and pulling the chain over his head. Instantly the howls and growls were replaced with words he could understand.

"The sky ship has returned!" the brothers heard someone say amid the jumble of voices. "Bring the King!" another yelled.

Jake glanced over at Scott with all his gear on and saw that, like himself, Scott was good to go. They looked like knights from the days of old. They were now wearing chain-mail armored shirts made from the strongest of metals. Their swords were made from the same super light and super strong ultanium material. Jake drew his sword and gave it a quick flick through the air. It was just as he remembered, fast and effortless.

Scott looked out the viewing screen expecting to see Nojo in the crowd. But he only saw Alserians gathering around the ship. "I still don't see Nojo," he said, with a hint of concern entering his voice.

"He's probably with King Bandilar," Jake suggested, while putting his sword back in the scabbard.

"Probably," Scott replied, as the two brothers walked down the ramp toward the throng of Alserians.

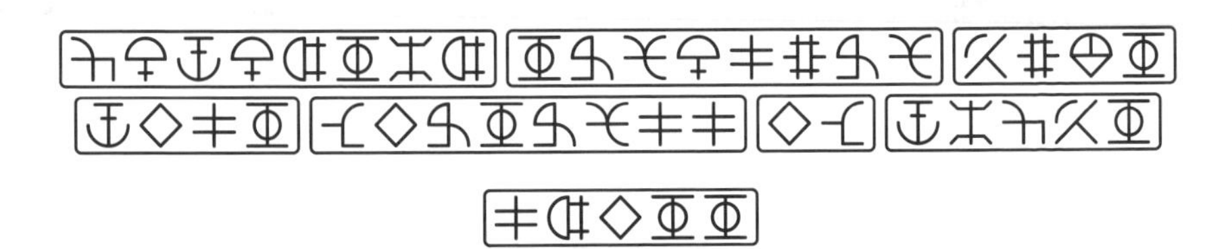

4 The Sky Knights Return

When the boys stepped out of the ship into the Alserian sunlight a cheer erupted from the crowd. They heard people shouting, "The Sky Knights! The Sky Knights have returned!"

Scott glanced at Jake and said, "They used to think we were demons. Now we're Sky Knights?" Then he thought about it for a second and grinned. "I like it."

Jake returned the grin and slapped his brother on the back. "Dude, we're Sky Knights now. So mind your manners and save a damsel in distress or something."

Just then the crowd parted to let through a small procession from the castle. It was Kefreti and King Bandilar.

"Kefreti!" both boys shouted and ran towards her.

"Scott! Jake!" Kefreti shouted back and ran to them.

Kefreti was squeezing both boys with all four of her arms in a big group hug when King Bandilar walked up to great them. He was wearing fine robes and stood straight and tall. “Great Knights from the sky, we are honored at your return,” he said with sincerity. “What brings you to our humble city?”

“That’s a very good question, King Bandilar,” Jake replied. “The ship came and got us, but Nojo wasn’t in it. Is he here?”

“No,” answered the King with a bit of concern in his voice. “He flew away in the sky ship that arrived with his warrior friends. But that was more than eight days ago now.”

"Hyper-Marshals? Were the Hyper-Marshals here?" quizzed Scott, getting all excited.

King Bandilar nodded. "Yes, he left with the Hyper-Marshals to capture Sinimak. But I fear we have not seen them since. His ship has remained in this courtyard until just a few hours ago. Then it disappeared and returned with you."

This was not what Jake was expecting. He figured Nojo would be here at the castle. Jake shook his head slowly and muttered, "This isn't like Nojo. Something is very wrong."

"You're right," agreed Scott, getting worried himself. "I think he's in trouble."

King Bandilar put gentle hands on both their shoulders, "I too have grown concerned for our friend Nojo. That is why I have already assembled an expedition of sailing ships to help him. But now that you are here, they are not needed. You can follow him in the sky ship."

"I wish we could," replied Jake looking up at the King. "But the controls of the ship are locked. It won't respond to our commands."

"Then we will launch the expedition, just as I'd planned," replied King Bandilar with finality.

The boys looked at each other before responding in unison, "We want to go!" Then they added as an afterthought, "Please."

King Bandilar chuckled, "Of course, of course you may go. After listening to Nojo's tales of you two, I would have expected no less."

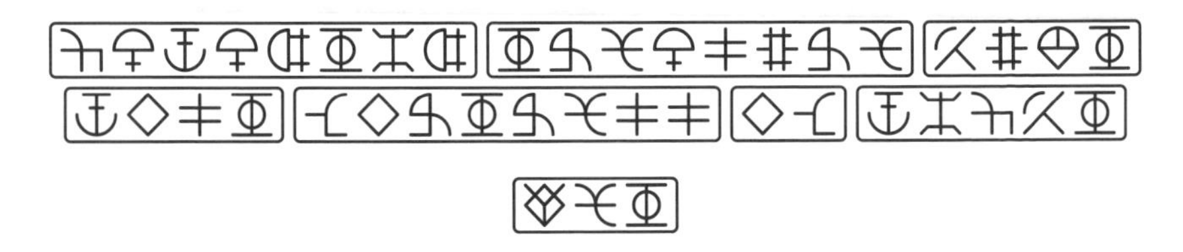

5 Where Is Nojo?

Jake still had many questions and he asked the king, "Great King, you said that you were assembling the expedition to help Nojo. Does that mean you know where he is?"

"I believe I do," replied the King simply. "At least I know where Sinimak went, and that is where Nojo and the warriors from his home world were going when they left here."

"Is it far?" blurted Scott.

"Yes, it is far, my friend," he replied. Then his tone turned very serious. "And it is a dangerous journey. The fortress itself is the most deadly of all."

"What fortress?" asked Jake. "Is Nojo being held in Sinimak's new castle or something?"

The King shook his head. "The fortress where Sinimak went and where Nojo followed belongs to no one in this world," he muttered cryptically. "The Fortress of Light belongs only to the dead."

“The dead?” repeated Scott. “You mean, it’s like a ghost castle?” Then he paused for a moment, recalling a movie he’d just seen. “Are there zombies?” he asked without a hint of joking. “I saw this Scooby-Doo movie with a whole island full of zombies.”

King Bandilar pondered Scott’s questions seriously. “As far as I know, those that have died at the Fortress of Light do not rise, nor are they ghosts. They are simply dead.” Then his voice lowered and he spoke slowly, “Everyone who has attempted to enter the Fortress of Light has died. Everyone!”

“Then why would Sinimak go there? Why would Nojo follow him?” quizzed Jake now fearing for Nojo even more than before.

"That is the mystery," replied the King. Then he suddenly seemed to summon confidence within himself and his voice grew firm. "A mystery that I know you and Nojo can answer when you all return safe and sound. The ships are fully supplied and can cast off at any time."

"We're ready to go with you right now," assured Jake.

"Unfortunately, I am not going. I am too old for such a venture. I would only slow you down." Then King Bandilar turned and nodded to a soldier that was standing behind him. The soldier was taller and more slender than most Alserians. "This is Tondir, the Captain of my guards," he announced. "He will command the expedition and watch over you."

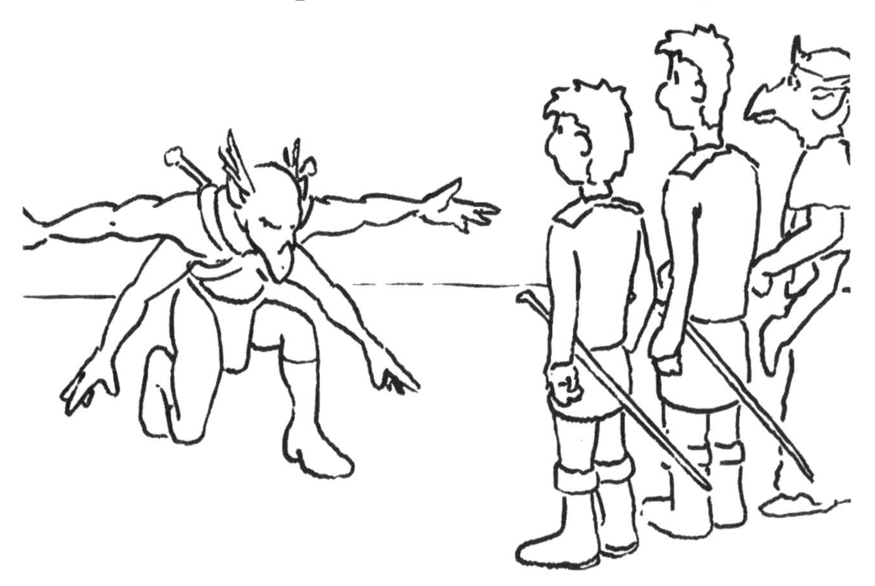

Tondir stepped forward with grace and swiftness. He was tall, slender, and athletic looking. He knelt down on one knee in front of the brothers. He bowed his head low, and his muscled upper arms were spread wide. "It is an honor to serve such great warriors as you," he said humbly. "Your powers and skill are legend in our kingdom." He looked them each in the eyes and said quietly, "I swear to protect you with my life, brave Sky Knights."

They could see the confidence and kindness in his eyes. They liked him immediately. Jake smiled at Tondir and replied, "You can call us Jake and Scott, Tondir."

Scott couldn't help but notice that Tondir carried no less than four swords. Two swords were on his belt and two more were crossed in a harness on his back. If that weren't enough, he had a small tomahawk axe tucked into his belt. "So, Tondir, why do you carry so many swords?"

Tondir smiled a knowing smile and answered, "One can never have too many swords, good Scott. Let us hope we do not need them."

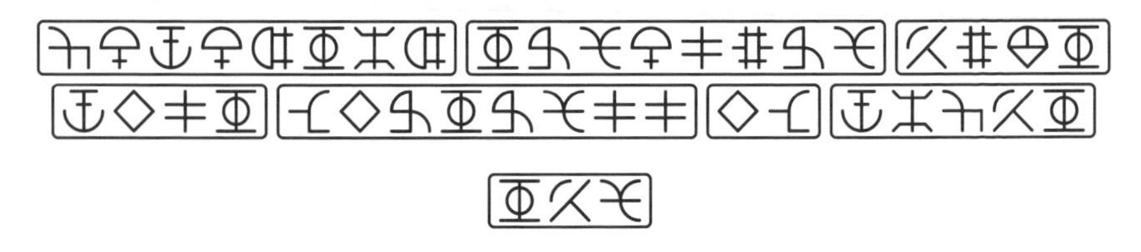

6 A Wild Ride

Jake and Scott walked down to the dock with a small procession of Alserians. At the wharf two large wooden sailing ships were lined up. They looked very much like sailing ships from the middle ages, only they were longer and more slender than the ships of old Earth. Their rigging was tall and their crews were at the ready.

King Bandilar led them up to the biggest ship and announced, "This is Swift Wind, the flag ship of my kingdom. It will carry you safely on your journey." Then he shook their hands and stood stiffly beside the gangplank.

Kefreti walked up and gave them big hugs. She whispered in their ears, "I wish I could go with you, but my father forbids it."

"It's okay, Kefreti," Jake called to her as they boarded the ship with Tondir. "We'll bring you back a souvenir."

"Yeah, maybe a bobble-head zombie," Scott joked.

The boys stood along the railing and tried to keep out of the way while the last of the preparations were made to depart. Within a short time a loud whistle blew and the sails were raised. As the two ships sailed away from the dock, the boys waved to the crowd. King Bandilar waved back, but they didn't see Kefreti anywhere.

A fresh breeze blew through the rigging, and the ships gathered speed. As they headed out of the harbor, the wind increased and the small waves that lapped against the hull grew in size. The closer they got to the mouth of the bay, the faster the wind blew and the bigger the waves got.

By the time the ship reached the open ocean, the wind was practically screaming across the deck. The waves had grown to forty-foot monsters of green water. The ship struggled up each huge wave and then surfed down the other side. Foam sprayed from the bow as the boat raced toward the bottom. It reminded the boys of surfing the giant tsunami off Atlantis. The main difference was that this rollercoaster ride happened over and over.

As the ship came to the top of a wave, Scott looked out over the vast ocean and saw an endless sea of enormous waves. “This is one crazy ride,” he shouted to his brother over the howling wind.

Jake stood next to Scott at a railing near front of the ship, almost at the bow. "No kidding!" Jake shouted back. "This is better than a five-ticket ride at the county fair!"

"Waaahoo!" both boys hooted together. "Yeehaa!" they hooted again.

At the sound of their hollering, Tondir ran across the deck. "Are you all right?" he asked with concern.

"Of course we're all right," replied Scott. "That's what we yell when we're having fun."

"Hey, Tondir," Jake asked. "Are the waves always this big?"

"Oh, no," replied Tondir. "They are normally much larger. We are lucky that the wind is light today."

"You call this a light wind?" laughed Scott. "This is practically a hurricane."

"The wind never stops here in the ocean," Tondir explained. "Once out of a bay, there is no land to slow or stop either the wind or the waves. The waves race clear around the planet over and over. In the stormy season they are the size of mountains."

"Thanks for explaining it, Tondir," said Jake. "It was a little crazy at first, but we're enjoying it."

"I am glad," said Tondir with a twinkle in his eye. "Now, I must go talk to the Admiral," he said and walked toward the stern, at the back of the ship.

Scott was looking across the deck to watch the crest of a wave pass by when he noticed something moving under the cover of a lifeboat near them. Then coming from within the lifeboat he heard a familiar voice ask, "Hey, Scott, is Tondir gone?"

7 Stowaway

"Kefreti! Is that you?" he replied excitedly, before adding, "Yeah, Tondir is gone."

Jake turned just in time to see Kefreti's face poke out from under the canvas cover. "Kefreti," he yelled above the howling wind. "What are you doing here?"

"I thought your dad wouldn't let you come," said Scott as both boys went over to help her struggle out of the lifeboat.

"He doesn't exactly know that I'm here," she replied. "Not unless he's already found my note," she added.

Jake whistled, "Ooooh, he's going to be mad when he finds out. I'll bet he sends another boat after you."

Kefreti shook her head and huddled closer to the boys, "No, he won't. I've thought it all out. These are my father's fastest ships. Now that we're gone, he can never catch me." She glanced around to make sure no one else on the ship saw her. "As long as the Admiral or Tondir don't see me, this ship will take us all to the Fortress of Light."

"You're a stowaway!" realized Scott. "You're a real life stowaway."

"I am a Princess," she replied. "I am the Princess of stowaways, so you need to keep me hidden."

"No problem," said Jake. "No one seems to come up to the bow much. You can hide in our room, and we'll smuggle you food."

"Speaking of food, I'm getting hungry," Scott added "I don't suppose they have chicken nuggets on the ship, do they? I don't think I could eat spider legs."

Kefreti laughed. "As I recall, you prefer to eat those peanut butter and jelly creatures. We have none of those. But the ship has plenty of fruits. I'm sure you will find something to your tastes in the galley."

"I hope they have ice cream," announced Jake licking his lips. "How do we get there?"

"It's toward the back of the ship," replied Kefreti. She started to give them directions, then shook her head, "It's hard to find. I'll have to show you, but I need a disguise."

They all looked around for something to cover her royal clothes. Kefreti found a patch of canvas lying in a box and Jake found a rope. Kefreti draped the canvas over her royal gown and tied it on with the rope. "There, I'm a deck boy," she announced.

Kefreti guided them toward the stern, along the railing. Soon, they went down a companionway into the belly of the ship. The boat creaked and groaned as it raced through the giant waves. They had to hold on to some part of the boat at all times just to keep their balance. Sometimes, when the ship fell off a crest, they would be almost weightless for a moment as everything fell. A second later they'd have to brace their legs as the ship crashed back down into the sea. The boys loved every second of it.

They came around a corner of the companionway and suddenly were face to face with a crewman walking the other direction. Kefreti bowed her head and turned her face away.

Jake said, "Hi. How are ya?" very brightly to the crewman as they passed.

The Alserian was so startled at seeing the fabled Sky Knights that he simply mumbled, "Pardon Sirs. Pardon," and didn't notice Kefreti at all.

"Your disguise worked great," whispered Scott.

"That's good," whispered Kefreti back, "because we're at the galley," she said pointing out the large open room they had just entered.

The galley had a kitchen at the far end with simple wooden benches and tables in the middle of the room. The galley chef in the kitchen looked up and immediately recognized Jake and Scott.

"How may we serve you, great Sky Knights?" asked the chef.

It was just then that Tondir walked into the galley.

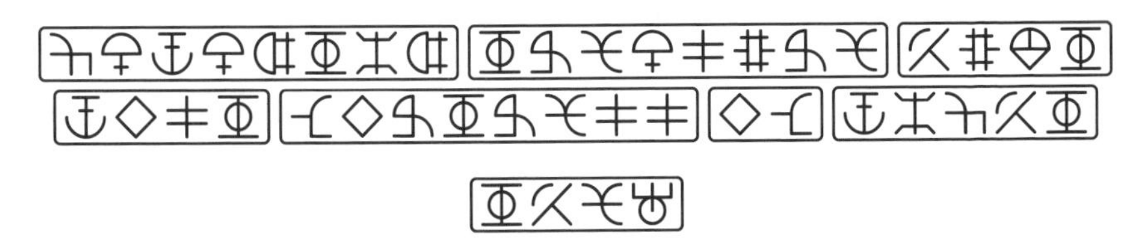

8 Moolish Pie

Kefreti instantly turned away from Tondir before he could see her face. As she turned, she saw a pointy hat with a long bill that lay on the floor under a chair. She quickly scooped it up and pulled it over her head.

Jake saw Kefreti's dilemma and covered for her by hailing Tondir. "Tondir, it's good to see you. We were getting hungry and this nice deck boy showed us the way to your galley."

Scott stepped in front of Kefreti to help cover her as well. "Yeah, we figured that since this whole ship is like a giant carnival ride maybe you'd have corn dogs and cotton candy," he kidded.

Tondir barely glanced at Kefreti when he answered the boys. "I don't know these corn dogs of which you speak. But we do have sweets, if you wish candy."

"Thanks," replied Scott in anticipation. "We promise to eat carrots or something healthy later."

"Our dad says, 'Eat dessert first. Life is uncertain'," added Jake.

Tondir turned to the chef and instructed, "Moolish pie for everyone."

As the chef went to fetch their pie, they all sat down. Jake, Scott, and Tondir sat at one table and Kefreti sat a table behind them, with her back to Tondir.

Scott raised his hand politely and asked Tondir, "So, Tondir, what is this Fortress of Light thing anyway? Why does everyone die there?"

Tondir pondered his answer for few moments before answering. “No one really knows the answers to your questions, good Scott. The Fortress of Light is a mystery that is wrapped in a puzzle and hidden inside a maze. It is ancient, yet it appears new. It can be seen for many, many miles. Yet, no one has ever been inside it. It is worshiped and feared. It was built by the gods at the dawn of time.”

Jake was about to ask a question when the moolish pie arrived. It was a sweet cream pie with a red filling that tasted like a super thick berry milkshake. It was delicious. After a few mouthfuls he injected, “Okay. So it must have been built by the Delphians. But what is it, a castle or something?”

"Perhaps," replied Tondir. "But like no other castle on Alsera." Then he put his fork down and a faraway look clouded his eyes. "I have only seen it once, when I was a young warrior on an expedition with my father. The expedition was led by King Bandilar himself," he added. "Along the journey we lost many men to the beasts and lawless tribes that live around the Fortress. When we finally reached the valley of the Fortress, it was like nothing I had ever seen." Tondir paused and squinted as if picturing it in his mind.

Scott could not contain himself and blurted out, "What is it?!"

"It is an endless flame a top a mountain. The mountain has four straight sides and the flame is fired by some magic that I know not," replied Tondir vaguely, as if he could barely believe his own memory. "The flame is even brighter than our own sun. Its light is pure green, greener than the trees. It shines only up, in a perfect line. The air around the Fortress crackles and dances from the power of the light. It is like a sword of the gods, piercing the heavens for all time."

Jake closed his eyes and pictured it in his own head. "It's a giant laser on top of a pyramid," he announced a moment later.

Scott nodded his head, “I think you’re right. But what about the Fortress belonging to the dead, what’s the deal with that?” quizzed Scott.

Tondir spoke slowly, “No one and no creature lives in the valley, for to stay more than a few days will make even the strongest warrior sick. There is a wall with four open gateways at the base of the mountain, one gate at each face. Each gateway is littered with the bones of many men. Our bravest knight tried to enter one of those gates. Moments after he entered the gate he was struck down by the gods.” Then a look of pride fell over Tondir’s face, before he added, “That knight was my father.”

“We’re very sorry about your father,” both boys said gently.

“Do not be sorry,” replied Tondir with no hint of sorrow in his own eyes. “Everyone dies someday. My father died as he would wish, fearless and on a quest for greatness.”

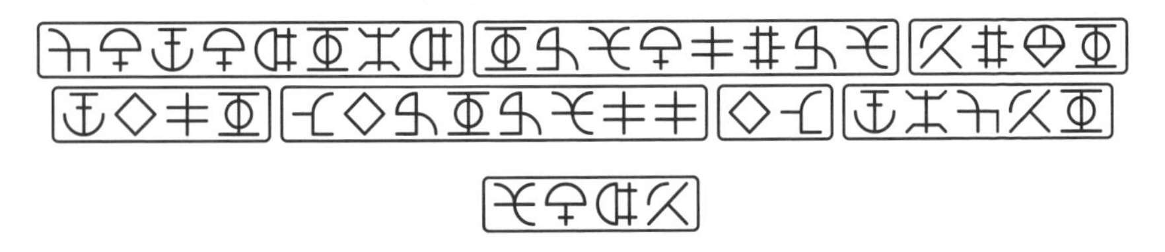

9 Life On the Waves

Tondir stood and nodded to the boys, "With your leave, good knights, I must see to my warriors."

"Of course, Tondir," Jake replied as the brothers stood. "We will be on deck if you need us."

When Tondir was gone, Kefreti got up from her seat behind the boys and joined them. "This is the first time I have heard such detail about the Fortress of Light. I did not know that my father had been there. It has always been shrouded in myth and secrecy."

"Let's get back up on deck before someone else sees you," suggested Scott.

They moved carefully back up the companionway in the lurching ship. Their thoughts turned to the Fortress of Light, and Jake thought out loud, "Now I know why Sinimak went there. The Fortress is an ancient city or maybe a way station for the Delphians. Sinimak is a thief, so there must be something he thinks is valuable in there."

"I just hope Nojo is okay," said Scott.

Jake patted his brother on the shoulder and replied, "Nojo is stronger than he looks. I'm sure he's okay."

Kefreti nodded, "I know it too, Scott. I feel it. Nojo is fine."

Over the next four days the two ships sailed on through the mountainous seas. The boys kept Kefreti hidden in their cabin with them. They brought her food and clothing to add to her disguise. When they all went up on deck to get fresh air and explore, the crew was so in awe of the two Sky Knights that no one noticed that a Princess was among them. Kefreti taught the boys Alserian card games and even how to use her Alserian yo-yo. Scott got so good at the yo-yo that Kefreti gave it to him.

Over those same four days the motion of the ship became such a normal thing for the brothers that they grew to anticipate the lurching of the deck without even having to think about it. They no longer had to hold on to things as they strolled along. Taking advantage of their super speed and super strength on Alsera, they would even use the motion of the ship at times to jump high into the rigging like acrobats. Their speed, strength, and daring never ceased to amaze the crew.

Tondir and the boys bonded over this same time as well. They begged him to teach them how to be better sword fighters, and he proved to be an incredible teacher. His speed with a sword could not match the boys', but his skill almost made up for it. They fenced for hours each day and with each lesson the brothers felt stronger and more confident.

In the early morning of the fourth day, the boys were up on the foredeck with Kefreti. The wind howled across the deck and foam rushed along the bow just as it had that first day, but now those things were ordinary sights and sounds.

Suddenly, Kefreti gasped and clutched Scott's arm. "There!" she exclaimed excitedly and pointed out past the bow.

"What is it?" responded Scott, looking into the mountains of waves but not seeing anything unusual.

"Not in the water," she replied, "the light in the sky. There is a shaft of green light in the sky!"

Jake looked where she pointed. He gazed past the jagged shoreline just a few miles away. Deep into the land he saw a thin line of pure green light going straight up. "I see it!" he cried.

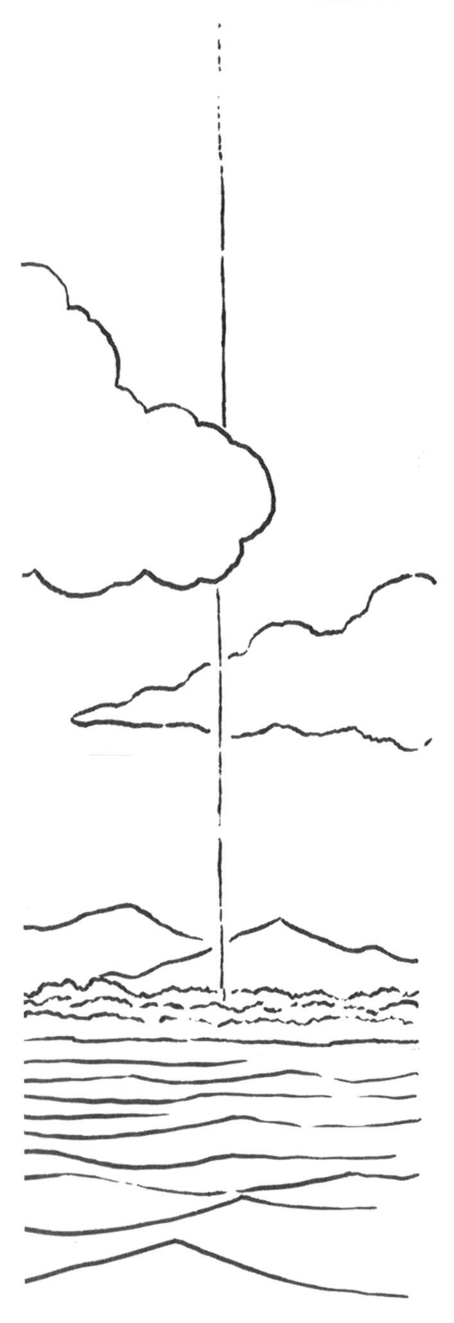

Tondir's voice surprised them from behind. "You have good eyes. That is the Fortress of Light. We should be at the bay where we'll land in a few hours."

Kefreti immediately bowed her head and tried to slip away, but Tondir looked straight at her. Then he put a hand on her shoulder, "Don't fear me, boy. I've seen you playing with the Sky Knights several times. Who are you?"

"No one, great Knight," Kefreti mumbled, with her head down.

One mumble was all it took. Tondir instantly recognized her voice. "Kefreti!" he yelled. "Is that you?!"

Kefreti simply looked up into Tondir's eyes and nodded her head.

"Are you insane!" he lashed out in a scolding tone. "Your father must be sick with worry."

But Kefreti was no longer looking at Tondir. She was looking just beyond him at the black object that flew out of a wave. "Dragons!" she screamed.

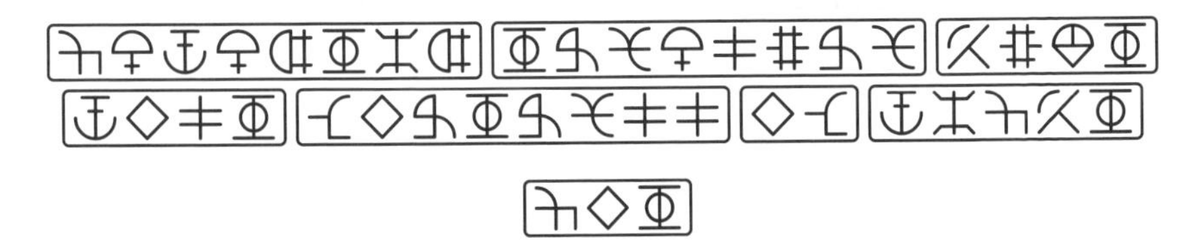

10 Something in the Water

Jake spun quickly and drew his sword. He saw something that looked like a cross between a dragon and a stingray leaping out of a giant wave next to the ship. It was four times the size of a man. Like all creatures on Alsera, it had six limbs. The forelimbs had sharp and nasty claws. The middle limbs sprouted stubby wings that tapered back to the rear. The tips of the wings had hooks instead of hands. At the rear were webbed feet and a tail like an eel's. But with all of that, it was the head that was most impressive. The head was on a long neck and had a mouth that opened impossibly wide to reveal row after row of very long teeth.

The creature was shockingly fast. It flew clear across the deck near the middle of the ship. In mid-flight it snatched a deckhand from the rigging as easy as plucking an apple from a tree. They barely heard the muffled scream of the doomed Alserian as the creature disappeared back into the sea with its victim.

"Battle stations!" yelled Tondir at the top of his voice to warn the crew.

The warning was too late for some. More creatures flew across the deck snatching crewmen as they went. The crew's screams were sucked away by the fierce wind.

"Everyone, below decks!" Tondir ordered, as he drew two swords, one in each upper hand. With a lower hand he plucked the tomahawk from his belt and handed it to Kefreti. "Use it well," he instructed.

Scott drew his own ultanium sword and put his back up against Jake's so nothing could catch them by surprise. "What are those things?" he hurriedly quizzed Tondir.

"Surf dragons," replied Tondir. "And there will be more."

No sooner did that warning leave Tondir's lips when Scott saw a black shape erupt from the wave directly in front of them and fly straight for the bow where they stood. "Duck!" he shouted.

The surf dragon flew fast. But Scott's high-speed atoms allowed him to watch it all happen in slow motion. As the four of them ducked low under the bow railing, he thrust upwards into the wing of the beast as it flew by.

The surf dragon screamed in a high pitch screech that was so loud it silenced the wind for a brief instant. With a gash in its wing, it crashed to the deck behind them and skidded into the forward mast. Far from defeated, it spun on the deck and turned towards them but didn't attack. It simply kept screeching, only now it sounded more like a call for help than a cry of pain.

Tondir pointed to the entrance to the ship's hold just beyond the dragon. "We must get past it and down bellow. We won't survive long on the deck."

Tondir ordered Kefreti behind him and cautiously moved aft along the ship's railing, keeping himself between the dragon and Kefreti. The boys brought up the rear turning their heads constantly, always looking out for new flying dragons.

The boys' caution was warranted. They hadn't made it halfway to the door, when not one, but two, surf dragons streaked out of the foaming ocean and flew into the rope rigging right above the door.

The surf dragons clung to the ropes from the hooks in their wings like bats in a tree. They were just above the deck and their long necks extended down allowing them to reach anything below them. An Alserian deckhand stood in the doorway, frozen for an instant with fear. In that instant one of the dragons struck like a viper. It snatched the Alserian from his feet and tossed him to another dragon swimming alongside the ship.

Scott saw that they were trapped on deck and steeled himself for a fight. He turned to his brother and said with some pride in his voice, "They're fast, but we're faster."

That was true Jake thought, but they still needed a plan of attack. Then it came to him. "Listen, everyone!" he shouted above the wind. "I've got a plan."

Jake explained it quickly. As he talked, the three surf dragons focused their evil gaze upon them and the dragons' mouths salivated in anticipation of a meal.

11 Battle Stations

Tondir was positioned between Kefreti and the wounded dragon. He drew his last two swords. He now held a sword in each of his four hands. Turning to Scott, he remarked with a crooked smile, “As I said before, young Scott, you can never have too many swords.”

Jake glanced at the ocean next to them and watched the ship rise to the top of a wave. “We’re almost there, Scott!” he shouted.

Despite the danger, Scott was still grinning in anticipation. They’d done it dozens of times over the last few days. It was always just for fun. But not today, today it was for combat. He bent his legs deep and waited for just the right moment. Then he felt it. The ship was falling off the crest of the wave. As the ship fell, he became nearly weightless. At that moment he jumped hard and simultaneously let out a war-whoop, "Heyaaa!"

Jake leapt at the exact same instant. His incredible strength on this planet allowed him to bound great distances even without the motion of the ship. But by timing his jump with the fall of the ship he practically flew. He felt like Peter Pan sprinkled with fairy dust.

Jake aimed his leap to land in the rigging just above the wing of the dragon on the left. He grabbed the rope ladder with one hand and simultaneously struck with his sword. He cut the dragon's wing hook clean off. The dragon lost its balance and swung down, barely clinging to the rigging with its other wing. Its forward arms clawed at the ropes to keep from falling to the deck. As it swung, the dragon's tail swept past Jake.

While he pressed himself into the rigging's ropes to avoid being knocked off, he warned the dragon, "And stay down! Because there's more where that came from."

Scott had jumped above the dragon on the right. When he landed in the rigging, he was too high above the surf dragon's wing to cut the wing hook. So he took aim at the nearest thing. His razor sharp ultanium sword sliced straight through the dragon's tail in a single whack. "Take that, you bully!" he yelled. The dragon screamed in rage and pain. It quickly pivoted in the rigging and started climbing after Scott.

Jake watched the severed tail flop to the deck below. Then he heard Tondir release a battle cry and saw the Alserian warrior facing the third dragon.

“Return to the deep, monster!” screamed Tondir as he rushed at the dragon on the deck. All four of his swords were in motion. He spun his arms in a circular fashion, one after the other. This created a whirl of steel in front of him that looked more like a giant blender than a sword fight.

The dragon cocked his head back, snorted, and then struck at this puny Alserian that dared to attack it. When its snout hit Tondir’s spinning blades, its jaw shredded and the monster recoiled with a howl.

Tondir wanted to press his attack, but he knew that his duty was to get Kefreti safely below. So as the creature retreated, he quickly pulled Kefreti into the doorway. The dragons were too large to fit through the door, so she was safe. But he stood at the entrance to help the brothers when they returned from the rigging.

High up the ropes the surf dragon with no tail was hissing mad and wanted revenge on the human above it. It charged up the ropes like a fireman up a ladder.

Scott scurried upwards as well, trying to stay away from the vicious teeth of the predator. The dragon's long neck thrust left, then right, hunting for a clear angle of attack. Scott used his sword to parry the jagged teeth of the beast again and again as it attempted to strike. Scott was fast, lightning fast, but he was starting to tire and didn't know how much longer he could fend off the remorseless attack. He began to wonder if this was such a great plan.

Scott climbed upward blindly, not daring to take his eyes off the creature below. Finally there was a brief pause in the attack and Scott glanced up to see that he was nearly at the top of the rigging. This was it, no where to run. He steeled himself for the next assault and taunted the dragon, "Come and get it, you big bully!"

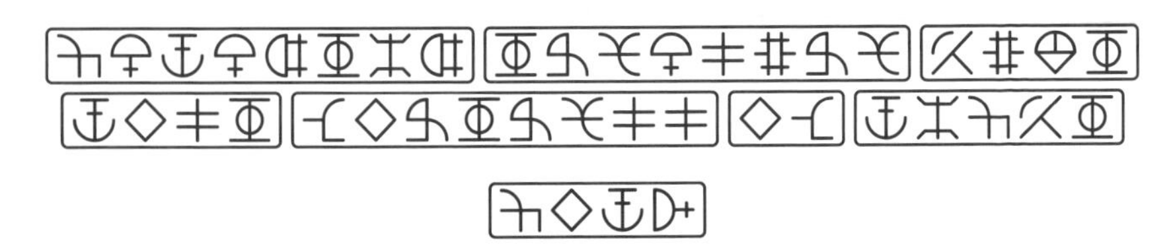

12 Surf Dragons Above

Jake could see his brother was in trouble. "I'm coming, Scott!" he shouted above the whistling wind and roaring of the dragons. Jake quickly sheathed his sword so that he could use both hands. He climbed so fast he was practically sprinting up the ropes. When he reached the left wing of the tailless monster, he pulled out his ultanium sword and yelled at the dragon, "Leave my brother alone!" Then he repeated his trick, by cutting the wing hook off this surf dragon as well.

The creature lurched as its wing hook was severed. It grappled the rigging with its clawed hands and tried to regain its balance. This was all the distraction that Scott needed. He hopped down one rung in the tangle of ropes and swung for a claw with his blade. "Eat this, squid breath!" he yelled, as his blow sliced off the left arm of the dragon.

The dragon now only clung to the rigging with the claw and hook on its right side. Its flippers were almost useless in the ropes. It lost its balance completely and swung away from the rigging like a door opening on hinges. The surf dragon's hatred of Scott was so intense, that even as it struggled to hang on, it snapped at Scott's head.

The attack was weak, so Scott simply ducked and said casually to the dragon, "Nasty Dude, you need to chill." With those words Scott took his sword and cut the single rope the dragon now clung to.

The dragon fell over backwards. It flapped its wings in a desperate attempt to clear the deck. But surf dragons do not fly well upside down. It impacted the railing with a bone splintering crash before sliding into the water.

As Scott watched the dragon fall, he also saw that the dragon Jake wounded earlier had recovered. It was climbing the rigging with a single wing hook and its claws. "Jake, look out below!" he warned.

Jake gazed down and saw in horrifying slow motion the jaws of the surf dragon about to close on his leg. Only his super speedy atoms allowed him to pull his foot out of the way in time. He quickly hopped up a rung and started to hack away at the attacking jaws of the surf dragon. "Thanks for the warning, buddy!" he called to his brother.

"I'll come help," replied Scott. He grabbed a loose rope that dangled nearby and used it to slide down to his brother in a flash.

With both of them standing side by side, the surf dragon didn't stand a chance of getting in an undefended bite. The brothers attacked the beast with their sharp blades over and over again. But the many cuts and slices on its jaw didn't deter the creature. If anything, their blades simply infuriated it. It bellowed at them with blasts of putrid breath.

Standing next to his brother, Scott's confidence had returned. "This guy stinks worse than Dad's toots," he remarked with grin.

"Are you kidding? Nothing is worse than that," Jake joked back. "But let's cut him loose anyway," he said, nodding at the two ropes the dragon held in his claws, as he added, "on three."

Scott understood at once. "Got it!" he replied.

"Three, two, one, now!" Jake chanted, and both boys simultaneously cut the two ropes.

Just as before, the surf dragon fell over backwards, flapping its wings in a frenzy of motion. This time the dragon managed to glide far enough to miss the ship. It splashed with a back-flop into the ocean.

From high up in the rigging, the boys looked down at the last dragon on deck. It waited for them at the bottom of the ropes. It had a hungry and patient look in its eyes.

"Don't these guys ever get the hint?" said Scott, tired from the endless battle.

Jake looked at the dragon and agreed. "I'm tired too," he admitted. Then he looked behind them at the sail and paused for a moment in thought. Finally he said, "We don't need to battle this one. We'll take the elevator."

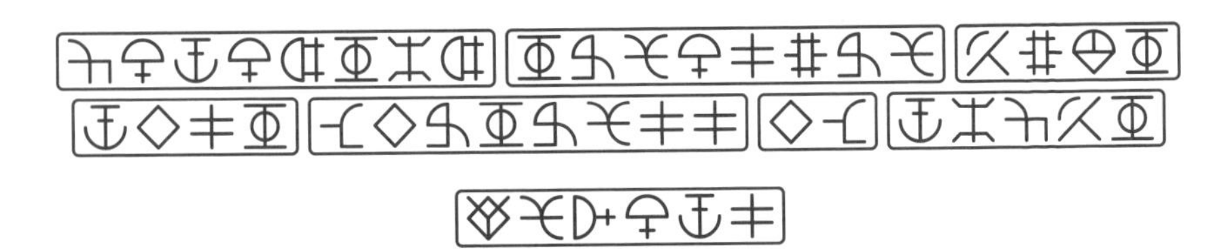

13 I'll Take the Elevator

Without another word, Jake slipped through the ropes to the sailcloth side of the rigging. The sail billowed at him more than ten feet away. He looked toward the deck far below and whispered to himself, "I've got to be crazy."

Less than a second later Jake leapt for the sail, sword outstretched in front. In midair he grabbed his sword hilt with both hands. He hit the sailcloth and simultaneously plunged the blade into the cloth. The sword pinned him to the sail and started to tear downward under his weight.

Scott followed close behind his brother, plunging his own sword into the sail to the right of Jake's path. Scott found that he could control the speed of his fall by twisting the blade so that the edge wasn't straight down. When he reached the bottom, he landed gently on the deck next to his brother. He immediately announced, "Now, YOU are officially the crazy one."

"You followed me," noted Jake, accepting the compliment with grace. "That makes you just as crazy."

Tondir shouted at them as he stepped out from the doorway, "Come quickly, crazy-ones, before the beast recovers his wits." He pointed at the surf dragon. It was still at the base of the rigging, but was trying to maneuver on its wounded wing toward them. Tondir added, "These doors are built especially strong, and they are too small for the dragons to enter."

The boys took Tondir's suggestion and sprinted for the doorway. When they got there, Kefreti hugged them both. "I feared you would be eaten," she confessed.

"We're not ready to be kid-nuggets just yet," smiled Scott.

"Then we need to get below now," said Tondir. "I've lost some of my crew. I'll need you to help man the harpoons." He started down the stairs into the hold saying, "Follow me."

They descended two decks into a wide open area that spanned the entire ship. Officers shouted orders and Alserians were scrambling about this interior deck. Many of the crew had arm loads of gigantic harpoons. Each harpoon was taller than an Alserian and made from iron. Along the sides of the hull were numerous square porthole openings. In front of each opening was something that looked like a giant crossbow.

"You take those two and I'll take this one," commanded Tondir, pointing at three loaded crossbows in a line. "When you're ready to fire, pull the trigger," he explained, standing in front of his crossbow and showing them a wooden latch that held the bowstring in place.

Scott stood where he was told and looked around. The whole place reminded him of movies he'd seen of pirate ships. The crew would stand behind cannons waiting to fire. This was exactly the same, only with giant crossbows instead of cannons. Scott grabbed the handle at the rear and experimented with his crossbow. He discovered that even though it was big it could be turned easily because it sat on a well balanced pivot.

Then Scott looked out the porthole and saw one, a dragon in the water near the ship. "Surf dragon!" he shouted. He gripped the handle and took aim.

"Hold your fire, Scott. Don't waste a harpoon on a baby," cautioned Tondir.

It was just as large as the others. So at first Scott didn't understand. Then it dawned on him, and he inquired in disbelief, "You mean, the surf dragons we fought were babies?"

"Yes, we must have hit a swarm," replied Kefreti, tucking the tomahawk into her belt. She picked up a harpoon and stood ready to help reload.

"Then how big are the adults?" asked Jake, not completely sure that he wanted to know answer.

In spite of everything, Tondir laughed. "Let's put it this way, they're not small." Then he added, "I'll be honest with you, if there are more than a couple of adults, our odds are not good. But I would rather live a bold and short life, than a meek and long one."

Scott nodded, "To a bold life then!"

Jake stood behind his crossbow and shouted, "To a bold life!"

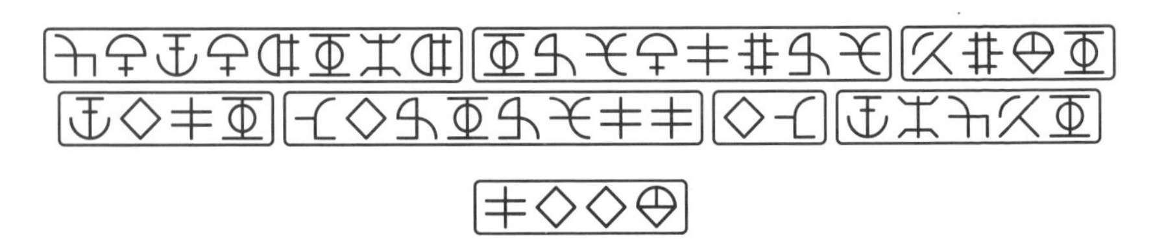

14 The Big Ones

Jake gazed intently out his porthole looking for something big. The other ship in the little fleet had closed ranks with their ship for protection. The two ships now sailed less than a soccer field away from each other for mutual defense. On both ships the decks were cleared, portholes were open and harpoons at the ready. Numerous baby surf dragons swarmed around them, yet none of the ships fired. They were all waiting.

Finally, Jake saw something. Or was it something? It was hard to tell. It was just a patch of water that looked wrong. It looked like the water had a giant hump in it. "Look there!" he yelled pointing at a patch of water in the center of the two ships.

Scott looked and saw the patch of water erupt with a massive dragon head. Its jaws were wide and the eyes glinted in the morning sun. Its roar was deafening. The beast leapt out of the water towards the ship just opposite their own. This was no baby. This surf dragon was as big as the boat it attacked.

"Now!" Tondir shouted. "Now!"

The dragon was moving away from them. So Jake aimed a bit high to allow for the arc of the harpoon and pulled back on the wooden trigger. The bow string sang out with a loud twang. Whoosh, the harpoon whistled through the air. It struck the beast square in the back, piercing the thick hide. "Yes!" hooted Jake.

Scott fired his own bow and he too got a hit. Dozens of harpoons flew through the air, fired by both ships. Many of them found their mark on the giant surf dragon. Yet, the dragon seemed oblivious. As Scott watched in stunned horror, it ignored the puny little harpoons in its sides and struck a thundering blow to the other ship with its head. The side of the wooden ship splintered just above the water line. The beast's jaws reached in through the hole.

"Reload!" ordered Tondir urgently, trying to pull the boys' eyes off the destruction on the other ship. "Fire for the eyes and throat if you can," he told them. "It is their only weakness."

"Here, I'll help you load," offered Kefreti quietly, placing a harpoon in both Scott and Jake's bows. Then she quickly helped them turn the crank that pulled back the string of the bow and set it against the trigger.

Scott set his jaw with grim determination and took careful aim for the neck of the beast. He fired and got a hit in the back of the neck. The surf dragon barely noticed, it still rained devastation on their sister ship. "You don't scare me," he whispered under his breath, but he knew that was not entirely true.

Jake and Scott both fired several more times, each one scoring as best they could. But the back of the creature was simply too tough. A second surf dragon, even larger than the first, appeared and joined the attack on the doomed ship. As the battle raged, their sister ship broke up from the constant beating and began sinking. There was nothing anyone could do about it. As the ship started to go down, the smaller surf dragon seemed to lose interest. It abandoned the sinking ship and turned straight towards Jake and Scott, then dove underwater.

"It's coming," said Jake more calmly than he felt, staring down the sights of his crossbow.

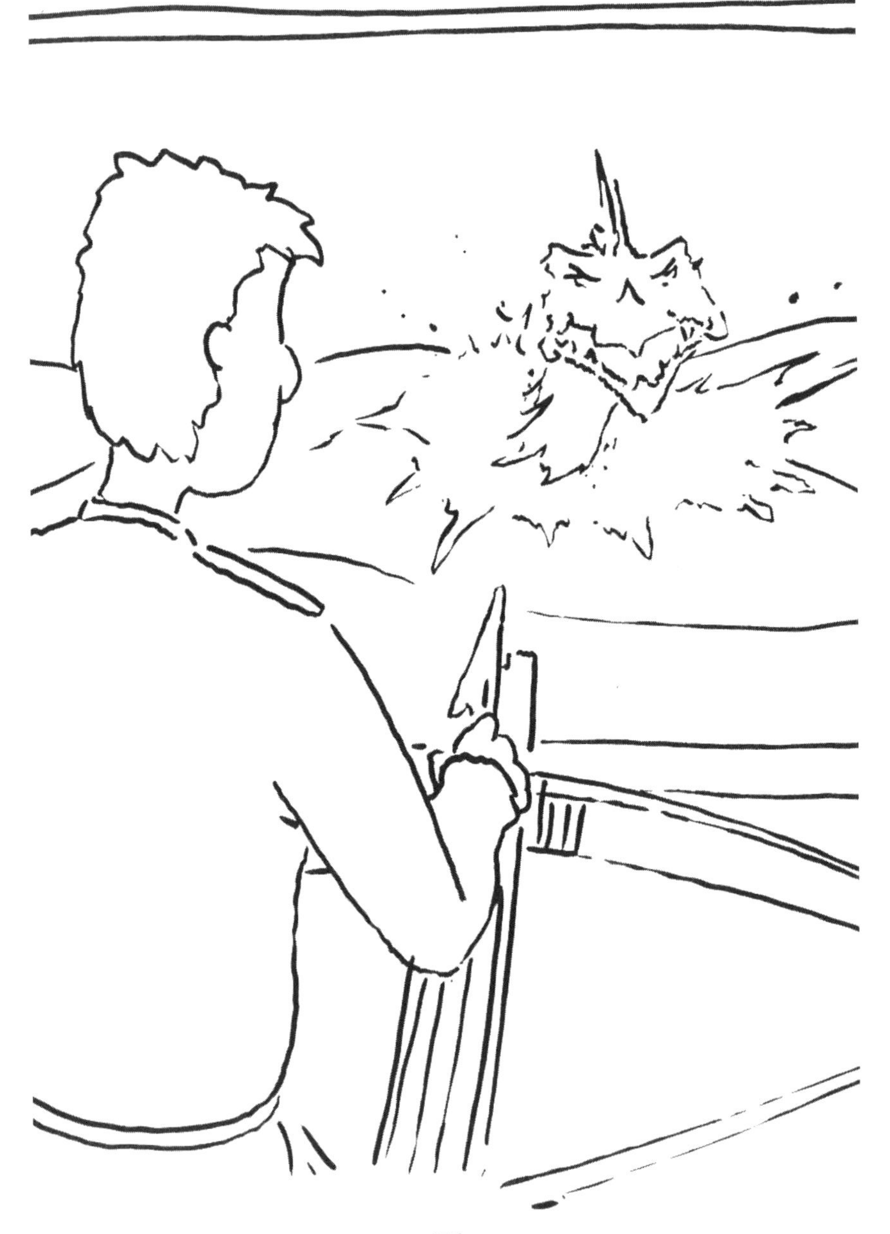

Scott finished loading another harpoon with the help of Kefreti and replied, “Yep, go for the eyes.”

True enough, a few moments later a gigantic dragon head reared up from the water. It bellowed so fiercely that they could feel the wind of its breath from many yards away. Harpoons flew from every quarter of the ship at the approaching monster. But Jake and Scott held their fire.

Jake watched the mighty monster approach. It was coming straight at them. Jake stared into those eyes through his sights and said to his brother, “I got the eye on the right.” Then he cautioned, “Wait for it.”

Scott adjusted his aim just a touch. “Cool. I got the one on the left. On your three count,” he added, calmly watching the mighty animal getting closer and closer.

The surf dragon was so massive, it looked like a jumbo jet flying through the water toward them, a jumbo jet with dozens of harpoons protruding from its back. Its sharp claws were held in front to grapple the ship it was about to attack.

Jake waited until the surf dragon was so close he could see the reflection of their own ship in the gleaming eyes of creature. Then he started counting, “Three, two, one, now!”

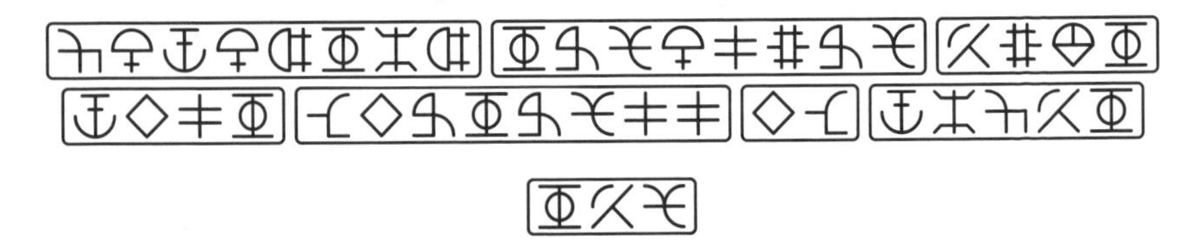

15 Attack on the Battle Deck

The thump of the two harpoons echoed in unison within the battle deck. Both brothers' aim was true. At such close range the harpoons buried deep into the black depths of the monstrous eyes.

The surf dragon let loose an ear-shattering scream and started flailing wildly in the water. It blindly grappled at its own eyes with its claws, which only blinded it further. Then it reached out towards the ship, still trying to grab its intended victim. But it couldn't see and swam in the wrong direction. It lashed out in a mad frenzy. It spun around and around, trying to latch on to the ship. A random swipe of its claws nearly snagged their boat as they sailed past the sightless dragon. When they were finally clear of the surf dragon, it must have sensed their escape and dove beneath the waves. It was gone.

There was silence for a moment on the battle deck. Then a cheer erupted from the entire crew, "Hurrah! The Sky Knights have done it. Long live the Sky Knights!"

Kefreti gave both the boys big hugs. “I knew you would save us. I didn’t know how, but I just knew it,” she gushed. “You are truly heroes.”

Jake just looked at his feet and mumbled, “It was nothing, really.”

“Mostly luck,” added Scott, humbly.

Tondir slapped the boys on their backs and said, “Well done, my friends. But it is not over yet. Look.” He pointed toward the water, and they could see the second, and larger dragon, was now in hot pursuit.

This one also headed straight for Jake and Scott. Somehow the dragon knew they were a special prize, the ones who had blinded its mate. Spray hissed from its nostrils like geysers. It was boiling mad.

"Time to lock and load," said Jake calmly, feeling more confident after their victory. "I got the right eye again."

"Roger that, Bro," Scott replied, as he cocked his harpoon bow. "Same drill as last time."

Only this time it was not the same. The surf dragon had other plans. When it was still a considerable distance away, it vanished beneath the waves.

Jake waited, scanning the water intently, looking for the head to pop up. He wanted to be ready the moment he had a clear shot on the eyes. Then he saw a shape in the water and knew in that instant their plan was doomed. "Below!" he warned.

Scott looked down through the porthole and saw the monster rocketing up from the water right next to the ship. The dragon's head was aimed just below their portholes. He frantically targeted the left eye. As he pivoted the crossbow, the harpoon hit the lower lip of the porthole and would turn no further. The dragon was too close and too low. He couldn't line up the shot. There was only one thing to do. "Hit the deck!" he screamed. Scott turned and threw himself at Kefreti, knocking her back from the portholes and onto the deck.

Jake and Tondir needed no urging. They were already diving for cover.

The side of the ship where Jake and Scott had manned their bows shattered with a horrendous bang. Wooden planks, crossbows, and giant splinters flew in every direction knocking down anyone who was still standing. Alserian crewmen screamed. The dragon roared. Its putrid breath filled the battle deck. It was chaos.

Jake rolled quickly on his back and drew his sword. He saw the massive head of the surf dragon thrust through the hole in the hull. The beast snorted like a giant horse, while its malevolent eyes searched the gloom of the deck for a victim. "The eyes!" yelled Jake to his brother. "We need to get to the eyes!"

Jake's shout instantly caught the dragon's attention. It snapped its jaws once in anticipation and then opened wide. Each tooth was the size of a dagger. Its mouth was bigger than a man. It could swallow him whole. The dragon lunged straight at Jake.

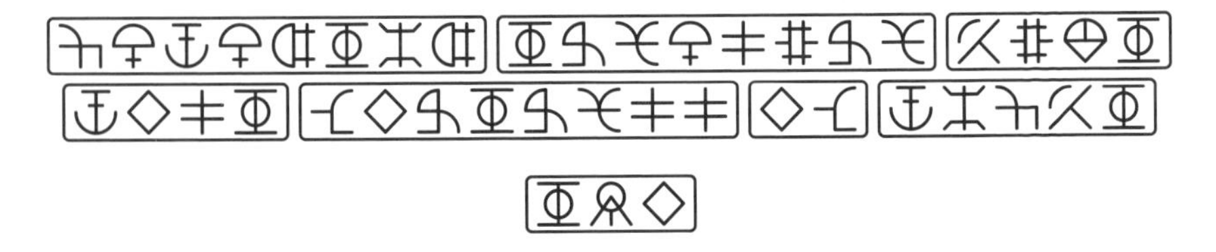

16 Destruction

Jake watched the dragon's attack in slow motion. He saw blobs of sticky saliva dripping like honey from the razor teeth and braced himself for quick action. Jake noticed the dragon was arching high, then angling down toward him. "The throat!" he thought to himself. "Tondir said the throat was vulnerable." He knew what he had to do. At the last possible moment, Jake rolled towards the dragon. He ducked right underneath the mouth.

As the attack unfolded Scott jumped up from the floor. He drew his sword just as the beast's jaw struck the deck where Jake had been a half-second before. The creature had never seen anything move as quickly as Jake. It was unable to understand where its meal had gone. Scott took advantage of the confusion. With incredible speed Scott raised his sword high and leapt straight at the right eye of the surf dragon. As his sword sliced into the giant eye, Scott cried out valiantly, "Live bold!"

At nearly the same moment, Jake rolled to a crouch at the throat of the huge brute. His ultanium blade swept upward in a curving arc straight through the neck of dragon. "Live bold!" he echoed.

The boys' blows would have killed a lesser animal. But they only wounded the giant surf dragon. It was now half blind and its throat gushed thick steaming blood. The dragon bellowed a sputtering roar and thrashed unrestrained. The hull and deck were smashed into pieces. The entire ship was disintegrating under the violent onslaught.

"Jake! Scott!" Tondir called out to them, "This way!" He was standing on the opposite side of the battle deck, pulling Kefreti with him. He shouted to the entire crew, "Abandon ship before it sinks!"

Jake and Scott both dodged the flailing monster and raced after Tondir. They sheathed their swords as they ran. It was almost too late, the deck was splintering beneath their running feet.

Scott saw Tondir thrust Kefreti out an open porthole then followed right behind her. As crazy as it all was, Scott could not help himself. He shouted to his brother as they sprinted for a pair of portholes, "Last one in is a rotten egg!"

They both dove through the portholes straight out over the deep green ocean. A heart beat later

they hit one of the giant waves. They had watched these same waves pass below them so many times, and now they were part of one.

When Jake surfaced, he saw Scott bobbing up as well. With everything they had just endured, the thrill of still being alive washed away any concern he had of being in an ocean of huge waves. "It's a tie," he declared.

Tondir swam up to them and his gaze turned to the stricken ship that continued to sail away, even as it floundered in the waves. "Few of us escaped," he said sadly, noticing only two other Alserians swimming in the waves. He pointed at the nearby shore. "Unless you want your crazy contest to end sooner than you'd like, you better get swimming. The baby surf dragons may still be around here."

Jake looked down into the water dreading the prospect of seeing a dragon. Luckily, all he saw was murky green water and sea foam. This small good fortune was of such little comfort that he quickly replied, "Good idea, let's get to shore."

Mercifully, the ship had been passing a point of land, and the shore was less than a quarter mile away. Scott looked at the shore and then looked at his brother. "Race ya," he said.

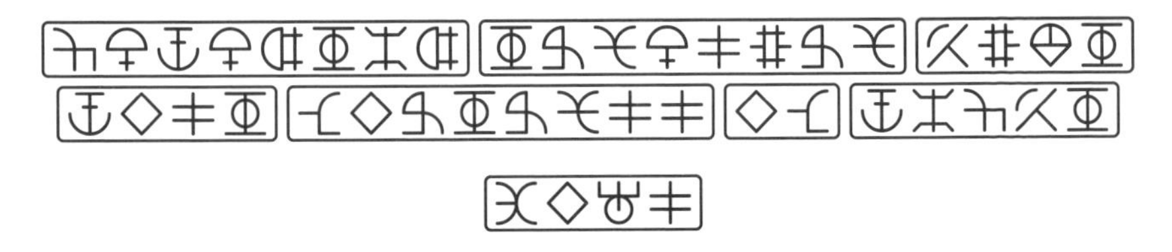

17 Land at Last

Jake was the faster swimmer, but he knew that they should save their strength. So after getting a bit ahead, he waited in the water for his brother. "Let's just call it a tie," he suggested graciously.

Scott knew he couldn't possibly beat Jake in a swimming race. "Naw, I'll give this one to you," he replied while treading water and looking around for Tondir and Kefreti. He saw they were far behind and remembered that even though he was slower than Jake, he was super fast and strong compared to the Alserians.

When Tondir and Kefreti caught up with the boys, they all swam at the Alserian's pace to the shore. They waded out of the surf onto the beach, lay on the warm sand, and soaked up the Alserian sun. Jake relaxed completely, closed his eyes and announced, "I could lie right here for a week."

Scott lay next to him and replied in a tired voice, "I could lie here for two weeks."

Kefreti laughed, "Everything is a contest with you two, even resting."

"Yep," they both chuckled.

Tondir stood up and turned slowly in a circle. He looked up and down the beach, and peered as far as he could into the jungle beyond. "I too wish we could rest here," he said. "Unfortunately, it is not safe. You see those?" he asked, pointing to some strange tracks in the sand further up the beach.

Jake sat up and looked. "Yeah. What made them?" he quizzed in response.

"Zulgey raiders," replied Tondir, "and they have manxwraiths with them."

"Why do I get the feeling that these raiders and manxwraiths are mean and nasty," said Scott, without even bothering to sit up.

"Because you know I carry four swords with good reason," replied Tondir.

Jake stood up. "If we're going, then, let's go. We still need to find Nojo, and I'm guessing that we'll want to be out of the jungle before nightfall."

"You are correct there," agreed Tondir. "I'll get the other survivors, and we'll go." With that he walked down the beach to where the two other Alserians who swam ashore were laying in the sand.

Scott stood up and helped Kefreti to her feet as well. When he looked around, he saw the beam from the Fortress of Light rising up above the trees. "At least we know which way to go," he noted. "Nojo is probably near the light."

"I think you are right," agreed Tondir returning with the two Alserians. He introduced them, "This is Reilig and Yamnix."

Reilig was wearing the clothes of a deckhand. He kept his head down and grumbled a short greeting. "Good on you," he said.

Yamnix was one of Tondir's warriors and stood straight and proud. His sword was drawn and at the ready. "I am at your service, great Sky Knights and wise Princess," he announced with a slight bow.

"We thank you both," replied Kefreti. Then she added softly, "We are sorry for the loss of your comrades."

Tondir pointed toward the beacon from the Fortress of Light and announced, "There is a trail heading in the right direction. I'll lead." Then he drew the two swords from the scabbards on his back. He turned to Kefreti and handed her one of them. "I see you still have the tomahawk, but you'll need a sword as well." He looked her hard in the eyes and commanded, "You will stay right behind me. Got that?"

"I promise," she replied simply.

Tondir glanced at Yamnix and instructed, "You're behind the Princess."

Yamnix nodded in reply.

Tondir turned to Reilig and held out a sword, "Here, you may need this. You'll bring up the rear."

Reilig shook his head and pulled a long and very sharp knife from his belt. "I prefer me own blade, skipper," he replied gruffly.

"As you wish," said Tondir before turning to the brothers. "You two follow Yamnix." He smiled briefly and added, "I'm not worried about you. With Sky Knights in the jungle, it is the manxwraiths that should be worried."

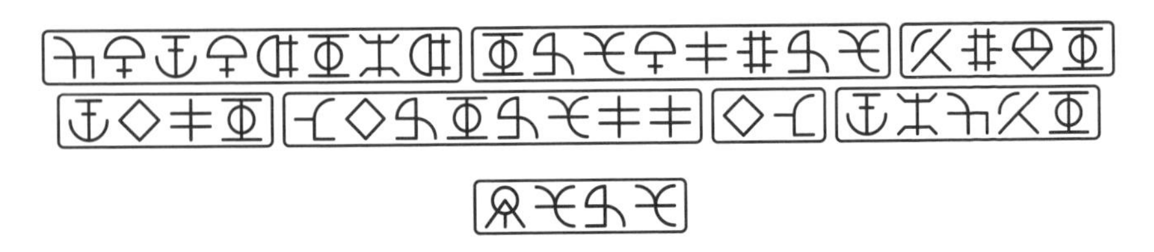

18 Manxwraiths Await

Jake followed behind Scott and they each drew their ultanium swords as they started on the trail. The jungle brush was dense, which made it difficult to see what was beyond the edge of the trail. All the same, Jake had this weird feeling that he was being watched. Yet, he could see no sign of animals. Then a thought struck him. He didn't hear any animals in the jungle either. That was odd, very odd. The only sound he heard was Reilig grumbling behind him.

"I wasn't even supposed to be on that ship," mumbled Reilig to himself. "I was just filling in for a sick mate," he went on. "And now I'm a nursemaid to a Princess. That's a fine fix, it is."

Jake knew he wasn't responsible for the plight of the poor sailor, but he felt bad for him anyway. He was about to turn around and try to cheer Reilig up when he heard a sharp whipping sound. Reilig's grumbling abruptly stopped and was replaced by the sound of something moving through the brush behind him. Jake turned and the trail was empty. The sailor was gone. "Reilig!" Jake shouted.

Tondir also heard the whipping sound behind them. He instantly knew what it was. "Manxwraiths!" he yelled. "Run!"

When they started to run, Scott had to go slow or else he would quickly overtake Yamnix in front of him. Yamnix ran hard, his sword at the ready, when a whipping sound erupted from the jungle on the right. A thick and spiky red line suddenly shot out from the brush and wrapped itself around Yamnix's neck.

It took Scott only a single heartbeat to understand what was happening. But that was one too many. He leapt forward and raised his sword to cut the red line away. It was too late. Yamnix was yanked off his feet and disappeared into the jungle.

"Yamnix!" Scott screamed. He stopped where Yamnix had disappeared and started to use his sword to hack into the thick jungle, searching frantically for the warrior.

"Keep running!" commanded Tondir. "There is a clearing just ahead, it is our only hope!"

Jake had seen Yamnix disappear as well. He stopped next to Scott and put his hand on Scott's shoulder. "He's gone, buddy. There was nothing you could do. I'll watch the rear. You stick close to Kefreti. Save HER!"

Scott took a final angry whack at the brush before realizing it was pointless. He nodded. "I will protect Kefreti," Scott replied, then raced after Kefreti and Tondir toward the clearing.

Jake had barely started after Scott when he heard a sound behind him. He turned to see something leap out of the brush and land on the trail a few yards back. To say it was the most wicked looking creature Jake had ever seen was the understatement of the century, and he'd seen more than his share of evil creatures lately.

It was about the size of a lion, but looked more like a big red scorpion than anything else. It had a fat bumpy body, with four legs, and two short arms with sharp claws. Its flat head and short neck reminded Jake of a bulldog, only the teeth were more saber-tooth tiger sized. But the mouth was not the most dangerous bit of the creature. The most dangerous part was the tail. The tail was very long and coiled like a spring. The tip of the tail was covered with sharp little spikes. Strangely, the beast appeared to be wearing some kind of leather harness.

"So, you're a manxwraith," Jake said out loud. "We want our friends back," he added while calmly sweeping his sword across his chest, ready to slash at will.

The manxwraith made no sound. It didn't rush at Jake, it didn't need too. Its tail started to swirl around like a rodeo cowboy spinning a lasso. A blistering instant later the tail was streaking straight for Jake's neck.

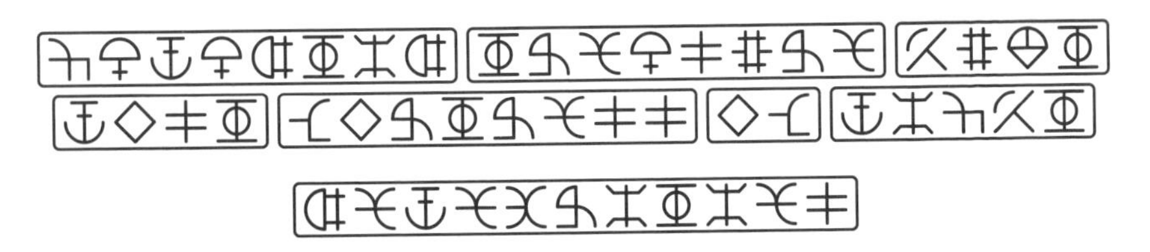

19 The Battle Begins

Jake watched the red tail coming at him in that slow motion way that he saw everything in this universe. The light gravity on this planet made it fairly easy for the brothers to jump rather high. So that is exactly what Jake did. He jumped straight up and pulled his knees up to this chest as he went. The wicked spiked tail of the manxwraith passed harmlessly just below Jake's feet.

Jake struck down with his sword while in midair. His ultanium blade neatly severed the manxwraith's tail in two. The tip of the tail fell to the ground while the stub recoiled back to its owner.

When he landed back on the trail, Jake glared at the wounded manxwraith and declared defiantly, "I'm not such easy prey, am I?"

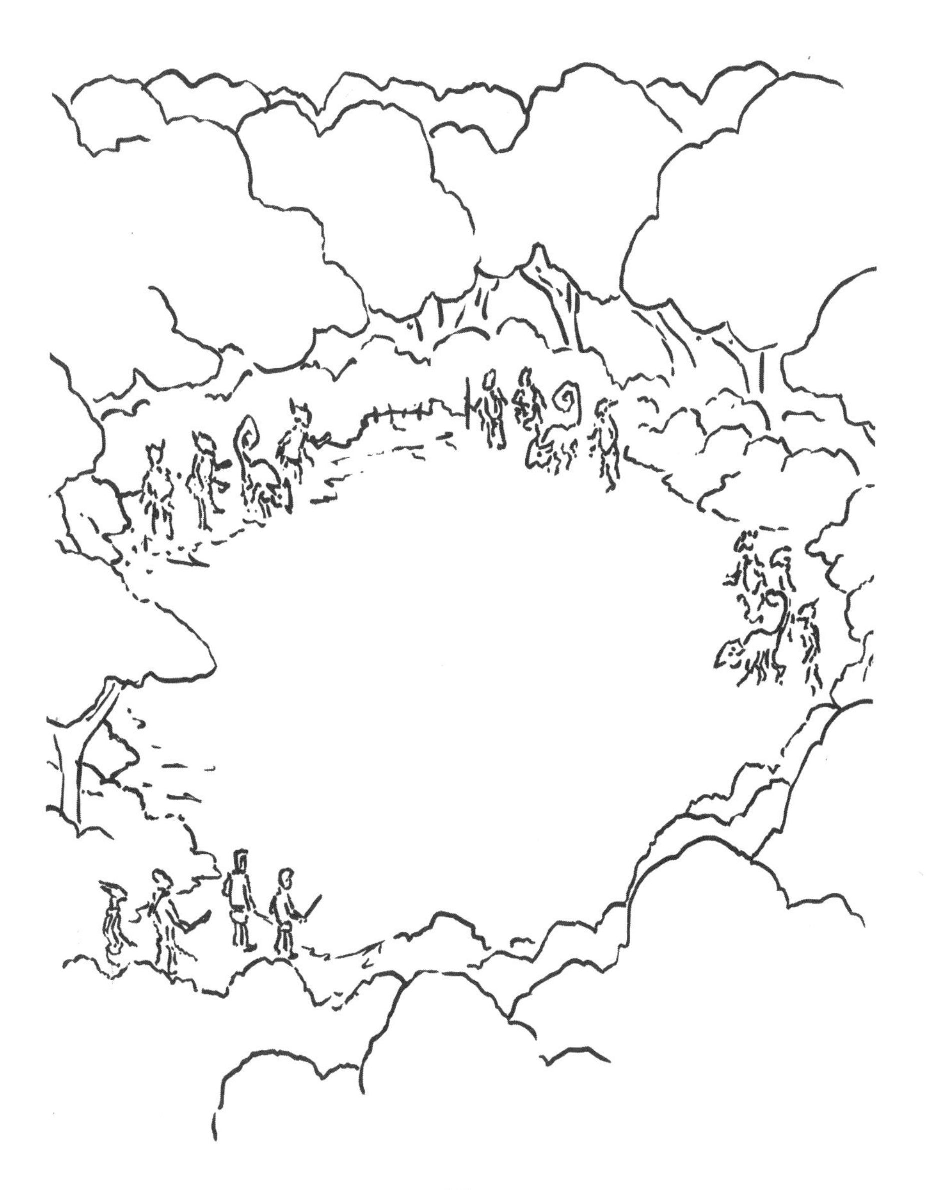

At that same moment Tondir, Scott, and Kefreti raced into the clearing. Scott immediately saw that it was not exactly the sanctuary he had been hoping for. At the edges of the clearing were three manxwraiths. One of the wicked creatures was on the right, one was at the far end of the clearing, and the last of them was on the left. Even worse, the manxwraiths were not alone. They were on leashes, as if they were dogs. Standing next to each manxwraith were three rough looking Alserians. "Zulgey raiders," Scott said to himself.

Scott was already running full tilt to catch up to Kefreti and Tondir when he saw the manxwraith on the right whip its tail straight at Kefreti. Scott didn't skip a beat. Without breaking stride he hurled himself at the Princess.

Kefreti saw the savage attack as well. She tried to raise her sword to fend off the wicked spiked tail, but it simply moved too fast for her. The tail zipped over her shoulder and started to curl around her neck. She didn't even have time to scream.

Swack was the sound Scott's blade made as it ripped through the manxwraith's tail. In that same instant he landed next to Kefreti. "You okay?" he asked, while he brushed the severed tail from her shoulders.

"I'm fine, thanks to you," she gratefully replied.

Scott growled deep in his throat and turned to glare fiercely at the wounded manxwraith. He shouted at the raiders next to it, "Take your wicked beast home before we make you!"

Back down the trail, Jake heard his brother yelling at the raiders and immediately realized that the manxwraiths were like trained attack dogs. That made them even more dangerous than a wild animal. True enough, the stub tail manxwraith he faced went on the attack and charged straight at him. "Wait for it," Jake instructed himself.

The thing burbled a sickening hiss as it bounded forward with surprising speed. It leapt straight for Jake's throat. Or, more accurately, it leapt for where Jake's throat had been an instant before. Jake was already below the manxwraith in a controlled fall onto his back. As the creature sailed over him, he thrust his sword into its soft underbelly. It screamed with an unearthly wail.

Scott heard the scream of the manxwraith and was turning his head toward Jake on the trail when he felt something wrap around his body. His arms were suddenly pinned to his sides. He glanced down and saw one of the long red tails tightening around his waist. He tried to raise his sword to cut through it, but the thick tail had his arms clamped in a viselike grip. Scott struggled to slip free. Even with his extraordinary strength all he could manage was to spin around to face his attacker. It was the manxwraith on the left side of the clearing.

Scott watched the evil creature gnash its teeth in anticipation of a meal. "This is not good," he thought, just as the manxwraith yanked him off his feet.

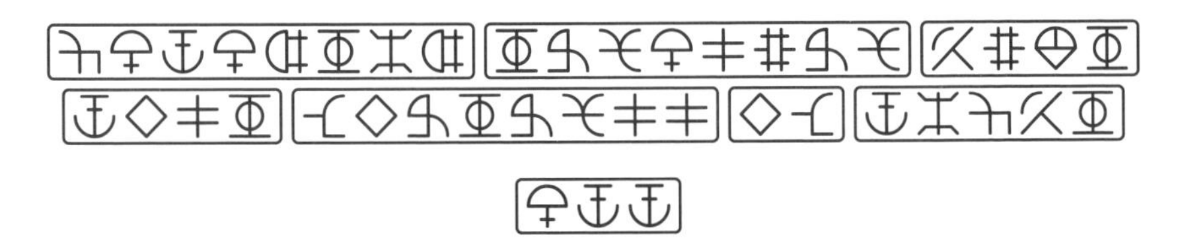

20 Battle in the Clearing

Even while airborne, Scott was not giving up. He jacked his feet around so he could give the manxwraith a swift kick in the teeth when he got close enough. It would be a desperate move, but he was desperate.

He was watching the jaws open in slow motion when he caught a glimpse of metal swirling past him. It was a tomahawk, Kefreti's tomahawk to be exact. It sailed over his shoulder in a perfect arc and planted itself squarely between the eyes of the manxwraith. The creature's tail went slack and it collapsed on the ground.

With the ease of an acrobat Scott landed on his feet and turned to look at Kefreti with astonishment. "Thanks!" was all he could think to say.

"Don't look so surprised, good Scott," Kefreti replied with a gleam in her eye. "I was Tondir's best student before you two came along."

Scott would have thanked Kefreti more if the battle wasn't still at hand. He had landed only a few feet from the dead manxwraith and its handlers. The three Zulgey raiders were none too pleased at the demise of their pet. They charged Scott with swords swinging.

The first raider to reach Scott attacked with a double-handed, downward stroke. After four days of sword practice with Tondir, the attack seemed incredibly weak. Scott simply stepped aside and sliced the raider's blade in two with his razor sharp ultanium sword. Just for good measure, Scott took a second blisteringly fast swing and cut what remained of the raider's sword off at the hilt. The raider froze in his tracks, too stunned to move.

The second raider let loose with a war cry, "Hi-yaaa!" as if he were a crazed Ninja. He started swinging his sword wildly at Scott.

Scott would have laughed if it were not all so serious. Instead of laughing he asked, "Are you done?" Before the raider could even reply, he took one step forward and cut the Alserian's sword to a stub in three whacks, so quick that the raiders could barely see the blur of his blade.

Scott fixed his gaze upon the third raider, who was still running forward with his sword held high. Scott shook his head in disbelief and barked at the fool, "What is wrong with you? Are you insane?"

The raider stopped in his tracks. All three of them stared at him wild eyed, their jaws dropping. They were dumbfounded by this Sky Knight.

"Go!" Scott commanded. He started to shoo them away with his arms, "Run away!"

This simple command broke the spell. They ran from the clearing and into the jungle.

Even before Scott had chased off the raiders, Jake had run into the clearing. He knew Scott could handle the raiders on the left, and Tondir seemed to have the manxwraith straight ahead on the defensive. It was the two raiders rushing Kefreti on the right that had him worried. He instantly sprang to her aid.

Kefreti was engaging the lead Zulgey raider with a series of smartly delivered parries and thrusts when Jake reached her side. Jake was impressed with her skill and complimented her. "Well done," he said casually. He then cut the raider's sword in half with a single slice of his own blade.

By then the second raider had arrived, sword swinging. Instead of cutting the raider's sword in half, he deflected it with his own. With another quick motion he stepped forward and smacked the Alserian in the side of his head with the hilt of his ultanium sword. The raider hit the ground like a sack of potatoes. He was out cold.

Kefreti seized the moment and attacked the raider with the broken sword with a vengeance. Jake merely watched as she made him back up a few paces before knocking the sword from his hand.

Wisely, the Alserian raider fled. The handler of the wounded manxwraith on the right followed this wisdom and also left in haste with his creature.

It was only after seeing the raiders run into the bush that Jake remembered Tondir.

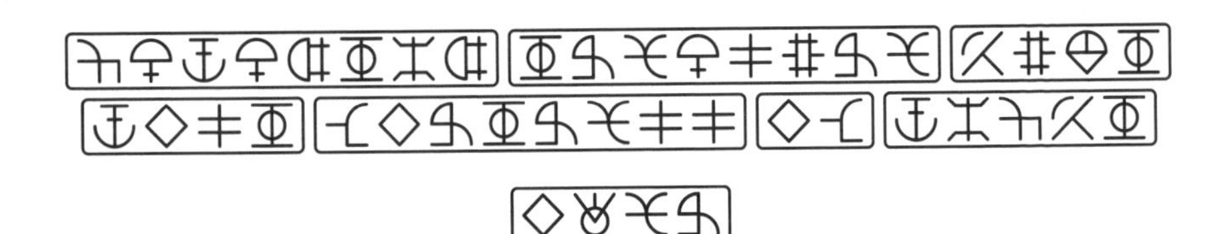

21 The Zulgey Chieftain

Having given one of his swords to Kefreti, Tondir was fighting with something of a handicap. Nonetheless, his three-sword buzz saw attack on the manxwraith was very effective. The manxwraith had already lost much of its tail to the endlessly swirling wall of swords.

Both Jake and Scott stepped forward to help Tondir, but Tondir shook his head. "This one is all mine," he said with a crooked smile as he watched the manxwraith preparing to pounce.

The creature leapt straight into the whirl of steel and thrust its claws at Tondir's swords, trying to grab them in midair. Its speed was so great that it managed to grapple two of Tondir's blades and knocked him off balance in the process. Tondir was falling backward with the manxwraith on top of him. But that was just as he had planned. Tondir knew the beast couldn't grab all three swords at once. As he fell, Tondir brought the third sword down hard. It split the beast's head in two.

Jake, Scott, and Kefreti rushed to Tondir's side and glared menacingly at the Alserian handlers, just in case they were considering attacking Tondir while he rolled out from under the slain manxwraith. "Don't even think about it," hissed Jake at the three remaining raiders.

Unlike the other raiders, these last three neither attacked, nor ran. They simply stood at the ready.

Tondir got to his feet and turned to the brothers. "I think we shall have no trouble with these three. It is the one behind them that will be trouble."

A clapping sound erupted from the bushes behind the remaining raiders. A big fat Alserian stepped out into the clearing. He wore a long black coat and a floppy black hat. The hat was adorned with jewels. He was clapping slowly and loudly. Clap, clap, clap. Finally he said, "Bravo, Tondir. You are as clever and skilled as I remember you. If only I had a hundred warriors so brave, I would rule the entire coast."

Tondir shook his head at the intruder before replying. "In that case it is good your men are cowards, Husmak. Even now that you're a Zulgey Chieftain, you can barely rule your own belly." Then Tondir's voice turned icy and he added, "As my father warned you years ago when we first met, keep to yourself and we will leave you be. There is no profit for you here, Husmak. Only graves for you and your men."

"Ha!" Husmak replied in mock laughter. "Tondir, your tongue is as sharp as your sword. But you are being rude. You have not introduced me to your friends. Are these the fabled Sky Knights that I hear stories of?"

Jake took a step forward and addressed the Chieftain coolly, "We are the Sky Knights, and we want our friends back. The one's the manxwraiths took."

Scott stepped up next to his brother and cocked his sword to his shoulder for emphasis. "And we want them back now!"

Husmak studied the boys for a moment before replying. "I have heard of your magic and I see the stories are true. If this were another day, I might even grant you your wish. But you see, I work for Sinimak now and his magic is greater still."

"Sinimak!" Scott blurted out. "Does he have Nojo?"

"Nojo?" Husmak replied before realizing who Scott was talking about. "Ah, you must mean the little grey prisoners from the sky ship. Yes, yes, he does."

Tondir spoke up, "We will make you a deal, Husmak. Return our comrades and show us where Sinimak is holding the prisoners. Do this and I will tell King Bandilar not to hunt you down like the rat you are."

Husmak laughed. "Nice try, Tondir, but it is King Bandilar whose days are numbered, not mine. When Sinimak gets what he wants out of those foolish grey men, King Bandilar will be no more." Then he smiled a very self-satisfied smile. "Sinimak has promised to make me the King. Apparently he has grander plans for himself. So, if you think your pathetic offer is worth your life, you are mistaken."

In response Tondir, Jake, Scott, and Kefreti all raised their swords into fighting positions. "It will be your grave we dig today," replied Tondir coolly.

Husmak didn't draw his sword. He simply raised all four of his hands to the sky and smugly said, "I think not."

At that signal, more than a hundred Zulgey raiders stepped out of the jungle and into the edges of the clearing. They were completely surrounded.

"Take no prisoners!" Husmak shouted.

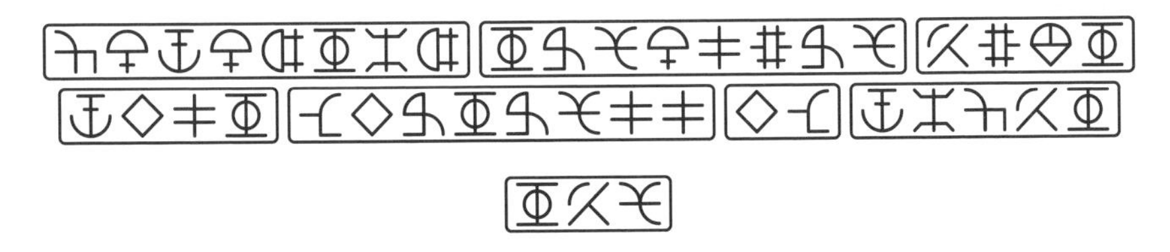

22 Surrounded

"Into a tight circle!" commanded Tondir quickly. "Don't break ranks for anything."

As all four of them rapidly maneuvered to stand back to back, Jake muttered a word of encouragement to Scott and Kefreti on either side of him, "We've faced worse."

Scott watched the circle of raiders slowly closing around them. He started counting the raiders. When he lost count, he added, "No matter how many there are, they're no match for us. We're Sky Knights."

Kefreti noted the amazing calm of the brothers and joined into the banter, "What is your saying? Piece of moolish pie?"

Jake watched the circle of raiders get tighter and tighter. The raiders started a low chant. They clanked their swords together rhythmically, bang, crash, bang, to scare their victims. But it wasn't scaring the boys. "Easy as moolish pie," Jake corrected her casually above the growing noise.

When the front row of raiders was only a few yards away from their circle, Scott cocked his sword to his shoulder with both hands and added, "When we get back to the castle, I'm going to eat a piece of Moolish pie bigger than my head."

Jake started to plot his first blow on the raider directly in front of him. "Come on," Jake thought to himself. "Just another couple of steps closer and you'll feel my blade." That was when a new sound reached his ears. It was a rumbling sound, or was it a sound at all? It was more like a vibration that he felt in his feet.

Scott noticed it as well. It grew louder by the second. The raiders stopped moving and froze in their tracks. The sound grew into a booming rumble coming from the left corner of the jungle. The expressions on the raiders' faces changed from wicked glee to fear. Scott couldn't resist the impulse, so he shouted "Boo!" at the raider directly in front of him.

As if Scott's silly "boo" was a word with magic powers, the raiders began backing up rapidly, then started to run.

As it turned out, it was too late for many of them. The left corner of the clearing erupted with the crash of branches. Even small trees were suddenly knocked flat as half a dozen giants thundered from the forest.

The giants looked something like an Alserian. The giants' faces and upper bodies were as Alserian as Tondir's or Kefreti's. It was everything else that was different. First, they were huge, the size of a small elephant on Earth. Second, they ran on four feet and had only two arms, making them look like a centaur. Last, they wore almost no clothes, and only carried large clubs for weapons.

Even without swords, the giants were fearsome in battle. The Zulgey raiders were scattered like toy soldiers under the feet of the giant Alserian centaurs. The centaurs' clubs, which appeared to be made from the stumps of trees, knocked entire groups of raiders out of the clearing in a single blow. The raiders ran in full panic from the onslaught. The few that raised their own swords to fight were tossed aside or swatted with a club.

Scott watched in stunned silence as the entire force of Zulgey raiders was decimated in a few short minutes. The centaurs had not attacked them in the center of the clearing, but Scott was ready. He had held his sword across his chest, trying to decide how best to defeat the centaurs when the attack came. As the last of the raiders were tossed into the forest by the creatures, he saw one of the centaurs turn to look directly at them. It stopped and stared at him. "Get ready!" Scott shouted.

Jake saw it too. The largest centaur in the group gazed at them with unblinking eyes. His head alone was almost the size of Scott. A cascade of bright red feathers adorned his head, looking a bit like a Native American headdress. Suddenly, the creature thumped his club once on the ground and started towards them. "Get behind us!" Jake called to Tondir and Kefreti as he stood next to Scott to face the centaur.

But their offer of safety apparently held no sway over Tondir. Holding his three swords high Tondir started running directly at the monstrous Alserian. He let out a war whoop and shouted his battle cry, “Live bold!”

In response, the huge centaur raised his own club high over his head and galloped straight for Tondir. As they came together, the creature bellowed its own cryptic war cry, “Fly to the sky!”

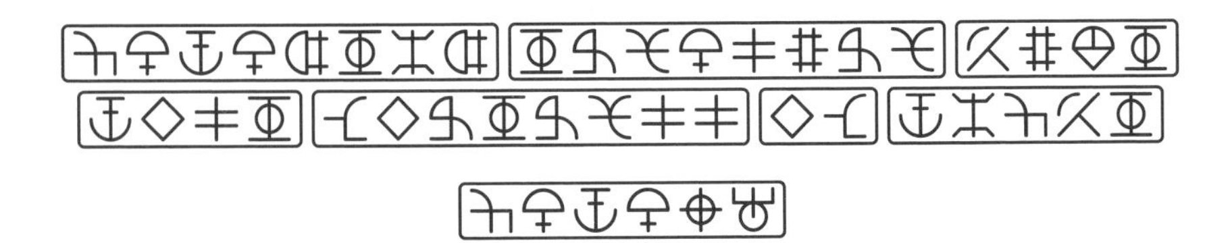

23 The Centaurs

Just a few steps from the centaur Tondir threw all three of his swords point down into the dirt. At almost the same instant the mighty centaur threw his club to the ground and reached out for Tondir. Tondir rushed straight for the massive pair of hands.

Instead of grabbing Tondir and crushing him, the centaur joined it's hands into a pair of cupped palms held low. Tondir leapt into the hands and was then vaulted high into the air by the centaur.

Scott stared in disbelief as Tondir flipped in midair and landed smartly on the back of the giant. It could not have gone any smoother if it had been an act in some bizarre alien circus. Scott let out a soft whistle and said, "Whoa."

Jake gratefully sheathed his sword and echoed his brother's surprise, "I definitely didn't expect that."

Tondir straddled the neck of the centaur and gave the creature a hug. "Fromuline, you old rascal. I am so happy to see you. It's been too long."

Fromuline answered Tondir in a deep but melodic voice, "But I see you have not forgotten our old games, Tondir. You always were the craziest two-leg I ever met."

"Speaking of crazy, old friend, I'd like to introduce you to my comrades," said Tondir from his perch on Fromuline's back. "I fear they are even crazier than myself, and that is not easily accomplished." Then Tondir introduced them in order. "I present King Bandilar's daughter, Princess Kefreti and the Sky Knights, Jake, and Scott."

Fromuline bowed his head to Kefreti, "Welcome, Princess." Then he turned his eyes on Jake and Scott. "I have heard of these Sky Knights." He smiled, showing his crooked yellow teeth. "It is a great honor to meet you. You are legend in the forest."

"You're the legend," replied Scott while putting away his sword. "Back in Mrs. Vetter's class, we read about centaurs, but I never thought I'd ever see one." Then he added gratefully, "Thanks for the help. How did you know we were here?"

"We ran into some raiders with a manxwraith and some prisoners in the jungle. After we dealt with the raiders, the prisoners told us you were here," replied Fromuline.

"Reilig and Yamnix?" blurted Scott excitedly. "Are they al right?"

Fromuline nodded, "They were banged up, but they'll be fine. I left one of my men with them."

"We're glad they're okay," said Jake. Suddenly, he realized that Fromuline might know something else. So he asked politely, "Fromuline, we are looking for our friend Nojo. He is a prisoner of the Dark Wizard, Sinimak. Can you please help us find them?"

Fromuline snarled at the sound of Sinimak's name. "The Dark Wizard is a plague on the entire jungle," he said. A look of disgust crossed his face and he spat on the ground, as if to get the taste of Sinimak out of his mouth. "His fort is only a few hours away. We will gladly take you, if it will help," he added.

"Thank you," replied Scott. "I can't wait to get my hands on that bug Sinimak. He'll be sorry he ever met us."

Fromuline motioned over three of his warriors and introduced them, "Sky Knights, you shall ride on Crystan and Syland. Princess Kefreti you shall ride on Prandlis."

Scott looked up at Syland. The mighty Alserian looked back. "Syland, this is going to sound weird, but can I request a favor?" he asked.

"Anything for Scott the Sky Knight," replied Syland.

"Can I try flipping onto your back, like Tondir?" grinned Scott. "That looked really fun!"

Syland laughed heartily. "Of course!" he said. "We can practice it as we ride along the trail."

Not to be left out, Jake and Kefreti turned to Crystan and Prandlis, "Can we do it too?"

The giants just chuckled and held out their hands. "Fly to the sky," the centaurs shouted. The next thing the three adventurers knew, they were flying.

24 We Need a Plan

After riding through the jungle for a few hours, the boys and Kefreti were becoming more skilled at acrobatics with their centaur friends. Kefreti could now manage a simple flip like Tondir had done, but the brothers were in a class by themselves.

“Ready, steady, go!” called Syland as he hurled Scott into the air for the zillionth time.

Scott rocketed upward and threw his head back before tucking himself into a tight ball. He was going for a triple back-flip. If he made it, it would be his record. He counted the rotations in his head as the jungle spun past him. One, two, three, now! He uncurled his body at just the right moment and landed almost gracefully

on Syland's back. "Yes!" he shouted, barely able to believe it himself.

"Amazing!" hooted Syland. "Never have I seen such a thing."

"Then watch this!" called Crystan, pointing to Jake, who was standing on Crystan's head.

"Yeehaw!" yelled Jake as he back-flipped off the centaur's head into Crystan's hands. Without a moments pause Crystan flipped Jake into the air, for a double front-flip and landed on Crystan's back.

"Your legend grows, my friends," Fromuline chuckled. "But we are nearing Sinimak's fort so we should stop here."

"Where is the fort?" asked Scott, from his perch on the centaur. "Is Sinimak at the Fortress of Light?"

"His fort is in the jungle, just outside the valley surrounding the Fortress of Light," explained Fromuline. "If his fort was any nearer to the Fortress, he and his soldiers would get sick."

"Can you tell us about Sinimak's fort, please?" inquired Jake, sitting on Crystan's back. "What are the defenses?"

"It is a simple wooden fort," replied Fromuline. "But the logs it is built from are stout and well set into the ground. The door to the fort is also very strong and can only be opened from the inside. Even we centaurs could not break down the walls or the door."

"Fromuline and I have been discussing this very thing," injected Tondir. "Sinimak has only about a hundred men. If we get in, I think that with the help of our centaur friends, we could defeat them."

"I have an idea," Scott said. "Syland and Crystan can throw me and Jake over the wall. We'll just open the gate from the inside."

Fromuline thought for a moment before replying, "That might work, but we'd have to wait until dark. They have cleared the jungle around the fort. The archers they have on the wall would see us." He bowed his head slightly, as if ashamed to admit something, "An archer's arrow is the one thing we centaurs fear."

"So we wait until dark then," said Tondir. Then he looked up at the sky and could see that the sun was still high. "It will be a while. We should rest."

"Hold on a second," said Jake. "I think I know a way we can get in there right now." As the plan formulated in his head, he began to smile. "Scott, you're going to like this."

After Jake told them his plan, all Fromuline could say was, "That seems impossible. Can you do this?"

Scott was grinning. "Oh, yeah. We can do this!"

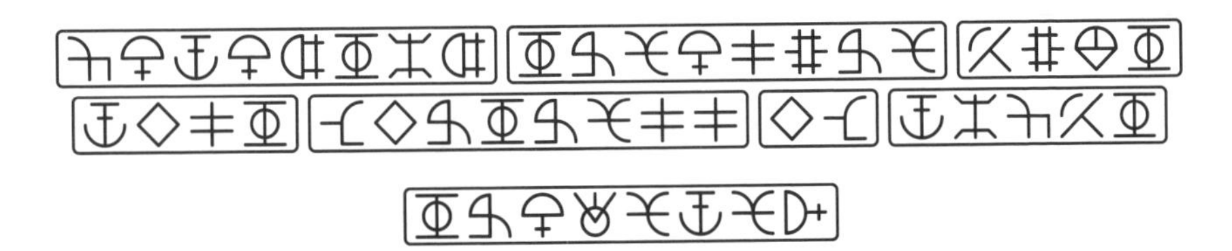

25 Sinimak's Fort

Jake stood hidden in the bushes at the edge of the clearing around Sinimak's fort. He looked across the open ground toward the wooden walls. He could see two guard towers, one on either side of the locked gate. Each tower held a couple of Alserian archers. "It's not that far, but it's going to be slow going," he mentioned to Scott. Then he plucked one last branch from the bush and tucked it into the band of cloth he'd tied around his head.

Scott was stuffing branches into his own headband. Now both boys' faces were well hidden behind hats of leaves. "Hey, bush boy," Scott kidded Jake. "I'm ready. Let's rock and roll."

Jake was about to fire a snappy comeback at Scott when Fromuline injected, "Your heads are now bushes. This I can see. But I can also clearly see the rest of you. I still do not understand. How do you plan to walk across the open clearing without being skewered by Sinimak's archers?"

"We're not walking. We're going to swim through the ground," replied Jake in a matter-of-fact voice.

"Swim through the ground?" echoed Fromuline, not sure he heard correctly.

Scott grinned. "Yep, we can swim through the ground. We can pass through anything on Alsera." Then he tried to explain, "You see, we're not from your universe. Our atoms move at a different speed."

"Atoms? Universe?" Fromuline repeated, before asking, "Are these magic words?"

"It's not magic," replied Jake. "We can move super quickly because the tiny bits, called atoms, that we're made from vibrate faster in us than they do in you. That also allows us to move through things in this world, but only if we push slow and hard on something. So, we can move through stuff, but it takes time."

Fromuline glanced at Tondir to see if the boys were just pulling his leg. "Can this be?"

"King Bandilar swears it is how they rescued him," said Tondir. Then he pointed at Scott, who knelt down and was starting to thrust his hands into the ground. "We are about to see it for ourselves."

Scott slowly pushed his hands into the ground. After pushing steady for a bit, his arms were buried

up to his shoulders. Then he started to pull in a kind of breaststroke, which slowly pulled the rest of his body into the soil. Soon his brush-covered head was the only thing sticking out. "Hey, this isn't so bad once you get the hang of it," Scott commented.

"Yeah, not bad," Jake agreed, pulling himself through the ground until his head was next to Scott's. "It kind of feels like wading through oatmeal," he added.

"Unbelievable," muttered Tondir, his eyes wide. "They'll never notice a pair of bushes approach them."

"Let's hope you're right," Jake said from behind his camouflage before turning to Scott. "Just keep moving, buddy, slow but steady."

"Race ya," laughed Scott.

Jake laughed back and the race was on. It was a race of turtles, but a race nonetheless. All the way across the open ground between the edge of the jungle and the fort, the two bush-headed boys inched forward together. As they raced, they taunted each other good-naturedly.

"You're slower than a three-toed sloth," whispered Jake to Scott.

"Oh, yeah," whispered Scott in reply. "I know worms that could whip you in a fifty-yard dash."

"Worms?" chuckled Jake. "The trees move faster than you."

Finally, the slow motion race was over, and they reached the gate of the wooden fort. No one had noticed them. Better still, the guards couldn't see them if they stood right next to the gate. So, Jake and Scott climbed out of the ground and took the bushes off their heads.

Jake whispered to Scott, "Okay, when we pull ourselves through the wall, be careful. Stick your head through first to see if anyone is around."

Scott was already plowing ahead. He pulled himself through the giant tree trunks that formed the gate of the fort. He could breathe inside the wood, and the air had a heavy pine smell to it. At first Scott couldn't hear anything, but when he was almost through the giant timbers, he heard footsteps followed by a gruff Alserian voice on the other side say, "Keep moving. Sinimak wants another word with you." Then Scott heard a second voice calmly reply, "That thief will get nothing from me." Scott instantly recognized the second voice. It was Nojo.

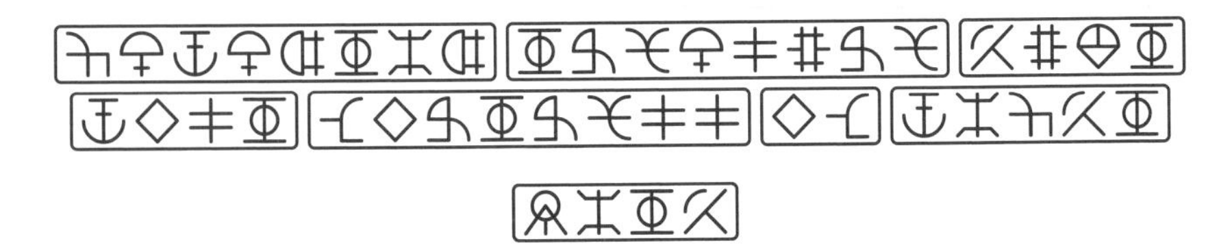

26 Past the Guards

Scott struggled through the wall and thrust his head forward. His face popped out the other side just in time to see two guards leading Nojo away from the gate down a dirt street. They turned to the right past a wooden building and he lost sight of them. "We're coming, Nojo," he thought to himself.

Jake's face popped out of the gate a few feet to the right of Scott's. He looked around quickly and was relieved that there were no Alserians in sight. "We're in luck," he whispered to Scott as he pulled himself the rest of the way through the gate. "Now we just need to take care of the guards."

"I saw Nojo!" Scott whispered urgently as he also finished pulling himself through the gate.

"Where?" asked Jake, excitedly looking around.

"There," replied Scott, pointing down the street. "They were taking him to Sinimak. We've got to help him," he added, drawing his sword.

Jake drew his sword as well. "We will, buddy. But first we need to take care of these guards and open the gate. You take the guards on that side," he said pointing to the left side of the gate. "I'll take the ones on this side. Do it quietly and meet me back here."

A determined look entered Scott's eyes. "They won't know what hit them," he replied.

Without another word Scott sprinted for the wooden stairs leading to the guard tower on the left. In the light gravity he could take the stairs four at a time. When he burst into the little room at the top of the tower, the guards were standing at the wall looking out toward the forest. They each held a bow, but the arrows were still in their quivers. At the sound of Scott entering the tower, they both turned. Their eyes grew wide when they saw it was a Sky Knight.

"How did you...?" sputtered the guard on the left, while trying to grab an arrow.

"Get here?" replied Scott, completing the guard's question. "I took the subway." Then Scott leapt forward and sliced both guard's bows into sticks with four swift strokes of his sword.

The two guards recoiled against the wall, stunned by Scott's speed. "Spare us!" They wailed.

"If you don't say another word or sound an alarm, I won't hurt you," promised Scott. "Now get down on your stomachs, hands behind your backs," he ordered.

The guards did as they were told. Scott used the strings from their bows to tie their hands and feet behind their backs. Next, he ripped a piece of cloth from their shirts and tied it around their mouths so they couldn't yell. Finally, he got down on the ground next to them so he could see their eyes. He put on his meanest face and hissed at them, "If I so much as hear a peep out of you two, I will be very, very angry. Got that?" The look in their eyes, told him that they got it.

On the other side of the gate, Jake crept quietly into the opposite guard tower. The guards were facing away from him watching the forest. Jake carefully advanced on them, trying to make no sound at all. He raised his sword above his head in a smooth motion, so as not to attract attention. He was four steps away from the nearest guard. Three steps, two steps, one step away when the guard sensed him and turned.

"Hi," said Jake brightly, just before bonking the guard on the head with the hilt of his sword.

As the first guard collapsed, the second guard turned toward the sound. Jake leapt straight at him in a move so quick that he was at the guard's side in less than a blink. The tip of Jake's sword flashed in the air and suddenly rested just below the chin of the Alserian. "Don't move and don't even think about yelling for help," instructed Jake.

The guard looked at Jake with eyes of fright and blinked frantically.

Jake backed up a step and said in a commanding voice, "Now turn around slowly and put your hands on the wall."

As the guard turned, Jake smacked him on the head with the hilt of his sword. The guard collapsed to the ground, out cold. "Sleep tight now," whispered Jake to the fallen guards as he left the guard tower.

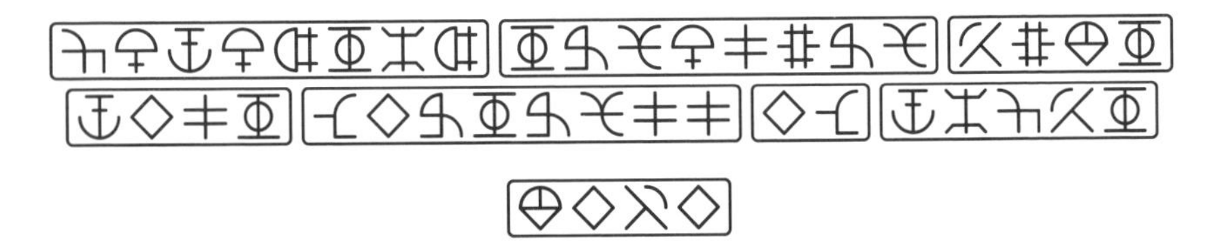

27 Found Him.

When Jake returned to the gate, he saw Scott already there working on lifting the big wooden bar that kept the gate locked. After Jake added his shoulder to the job they quickly dropped the bar onto the ground and pushed the wooden doors open. No other signal was needed. Kefreti, Tondir, and the centaurs started charging across the clearing.

"Let's find Nojo before this place goes nuts," said Jake, turning back into the fort.

"They went this way," replied Scott, drawing his sword and starting to trot down the dirt street.

Their luck held and they didn't meet any of Sinimak's soldiers. When they got to the spot where Scott had lost sight of Nojo, Scott said, "They turned down this street. Come on."

After only a few yards, Jake raised his hand. "Hold up a second," he cautioned. "I think I hear someone."

Scott stopped in his tracks and listened quietly for a moment. He heard it too. Voices came from a doorway in the building on his right. He stepped closer to the door and recognized the voice. It was Sinimak.

"I'm losing my patience, Nojolani," Sinimak snarled. His croaky voice was followed by the sound of a hand slapping flesh. "I know you have the key. How else could you open the vault under Bandilar's castle? Now, where is it?"

Nojo ignored the throbbing in his cheek, where he'd been slapped. "How many times do I have to tell you," he replied firmly, "I have no idea what you're talking about."

"You may not be able to play this game much longer," Sinimak warned. "My spies tell me those Earth boys showed up in your starship. I'll bet they know where the key is. When I'm through with them, they will talk."

"Leave them alone! They know nothing," Nojo burst out. "They're just my friends." Then Nojo's voice turned menacing, "If you touch them, I swear I'll hunt you to the ends of all the universes."

Sinimak just cackled at Nojo, "When I get the Pillar of Knowledge, I will rule every universe!" Then Sinimak suddenly stopped. He had heard a rumbling sound. It was the sound of the centaurs charging through the open gate.

That was Jake and Scott's cue. They burst through the door. When they entered the room, Scott moved left and Jake moved to the right. In the center of the room Sinimak was standing over Nojo. Nojo was tied with rope to a chair.

"All you're going to rule is a jail for worms, you worm!" barked Scott at Sinimak.

"Step away from Nojo," added Jake firmly. Then he raised his sword to a fighting position as a warning. "I mean, now!"

Jake and Scott were used to seeing things happen in slow motion in this universe. What they had forgotten was that Sinimak was also from another universe. His movements were fast, faster than they expected. He reached into his pocket, pulled out a gravity wand and waved it at Jake. "No! You step back, child!" he cackled.

"Jake! Watch out!" Nojo warned. But it was too late.

Sinimak's gravity wand was more powerful than the one that Nojo carried. Jake felt like he was given a karate kick in the chest. He was thrown back against a wall and pinned there for a moment, before falling to the ground. "Get him!" Jake managed to yell to Scott.

Scott was already launching his attack. He jumped forward, his sword sweeping in an arc to knock the wand from Sinimak's hand. He let out a yell like a samurai on the attack. "Yaaaaa!"

With a mere flick of his wrist, Sinimak adjusted the aim of his gravity beam. It stopped Scott in his tracks and threw him toward the left wall. Scott slammed into a table near the wall. The impact from his body broke one of the table legs, and Scott's sword clattered to the ground. An instant later, both Scott and the table crashed to the dirt floor of the room.

"Guards!" screamed Sinimak at the top of his lungs.

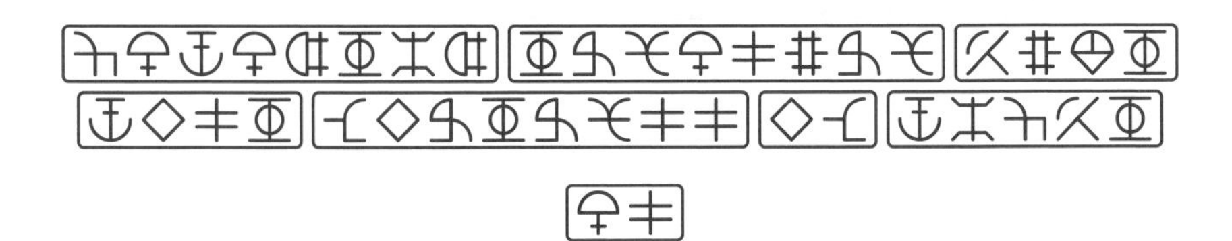

28 Sinimak's Defeat

Sinimak's call for guards was answered by the sound of shouts, yells, running feet, and splintering wood. The problem for Sinimak was that the sounds were not coming from guards rushing to save him. The sounds were coming from his soldiers fleeing from the attack by Tondir, Kefreti, and the centaurs.

Jake listened to the horrendous crack of a centaur's giant club as it smashed into a building near them. He grinned. "I think our reinforcements have arrived," he said to Sinimak, while picking himself up off the ground. "Your little army will soon be defeated, just like your raider friends were destroyed."

Sinimak stood directly in front of Nojo and glared at both Jake and Scott. He waved his gravity wand menacingly at both boys, but his hand was starting to tremble. "Don't move or I'll crush you like a bug!" he hissed.

Scott stood behind the fallen table. "A bug?" he shot back. "Those centaurs will crush you like a bug in about one minute."

“Fool!” Sinimak responded. “The gravity wand works on those giants just as well. The bigger they are, the harder they fall,” he laughed in a shrill voice.

When Scott stood up, he kept his right hand below the edge of the table where Sinimak couldn’t see it, but Jake could tell what Scott was up to. Jake knew that he needed to get Sinimak’s full attention. “You’re little gravity tricks don’t scare me,” Jake announced loudly. Then he raised his sword and stepped forward.

Sinimak aimed his gravity wand to push Jake backward. At that exact same instant Scott's right hand came up from behind the table. It held the broken table leg. As Jake was slammed backward by Sinimak's gravity beam, Scott threw the chunk of wood at Sinimak's wand. Scott's throw was perfect. The wand flew from Sinimak's hand.

"No!" Sinimak screamed, even as he started to dive for the wand.

Nojo knew the boys would try something, so he was prepared. He strained against his ropes and rocked forward in the chair. He gave Sinimak a head-butt in the back just as Sinimak was reaching for the wand. The impact threw off Sinimak's aim and he sprawled onto the ground.

Scott leapt over the table and snatched the gravity wand out of the dirt before Sinimak could grab it.

Jake had been ready for the gravity kick this time, so he recovered quickly. In an instant, he charged forward and pointed his blade right at Sinimak's neck. "Stay down and don't even think about trying anything," he warned.

Scott picked his own sword up out of the dirt and used it to quickly cut the ropes around Nojo. "It's good to see you, Nojo," Scott said brightly, handing Nojo the gravity wand Sinimak dropped. "We were worried about you."

Nojo got up from his chair and gave each of the boys a big hug, while keeping an eye on Sinimak the whole time. "Boys, you have no idea how wonderful it is to see you," Nojo said warmly. A giant smile spread across his face. Then he added in a fatherly tone, "But you shouldn't have come. It's very dangerous here."

Both boys started to laugh, "Yeah, we noticed that."

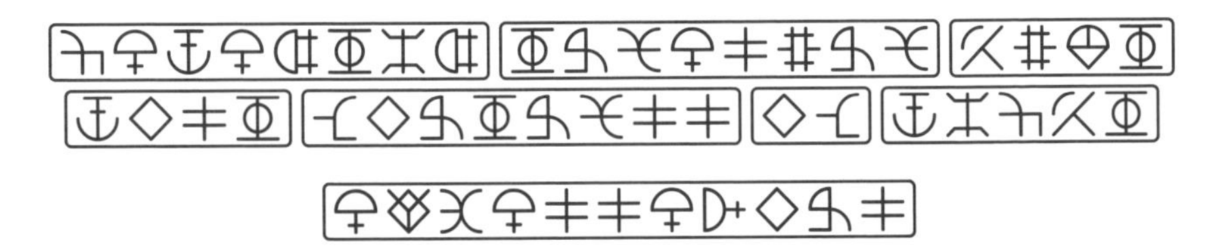

29 Nojo's Tale

Jake kept his sword on Sinimak as he asked the question that had been bugging him ever since they got to Alsera, "So, Nojo, King Bandilar told us that you came here with the Hyper-Marshals. I thought the Hyper-Marshals were like high tech commandos. How did Sinimak capture you?"

Nojo gave a withering glance at Sinimak. "Treachery of course," Nojo replied simply. Then he explained further, "We flew here in Lieutenant Zyperion's Hyper-Marshal ship and found this fort straightaway. That starship could have blasted this place into a rubbish pile in a nano-second, but we didn't want to harm the Alserians. So, when Sinimak and a few dozen soldiers hightailed it out of here, we followed right above them in the ship toward the Fortress of Light. The whole time we kept warning Sinimak's soldiers to lay down their weapons or be destroyed."

"So, what did they do?" asked Scott.

"That was the deceptive part," replied Nojo. "They didn't do a ruddy thing. They just rode the short distance into the barren valley surrounding the Fortress of Light. But Sinimak new something we didn't know. The Fortress of Light puts out some kind of space-time field that shut down everything on our ship. If we hadn't been just a few feet off the ground when we crossed into that valley, we'd have all been killed in the crash. As it was, we hit pretty hard, but we all survived and so did the ship. Within seconds of the crash Sinimak and his men broke in through a door and took us prisoner."

"We're glad you weren't hurt in the crash," said Jake. "So, what happened to the Hyper-Marshals and their ship? Is it still at the crash site?"

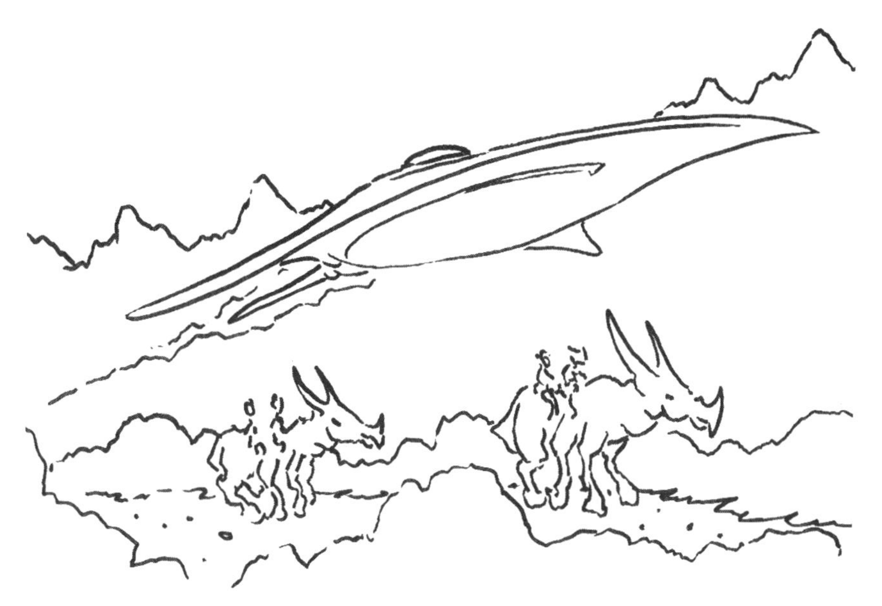

"Zyperion, his Hyper-Marshals, and I have been prisoners in a pit at the far end of the fort. But I heard the guards talking, and I gather Sinimak's men used beasts to drag the ship out of the valley and back into the forest. So it might work again," replied Nojo. Then he narrowed his eyes at Sinimak. "This thief has been trying to fix it these last few days. Haven't you, Sinimak?"

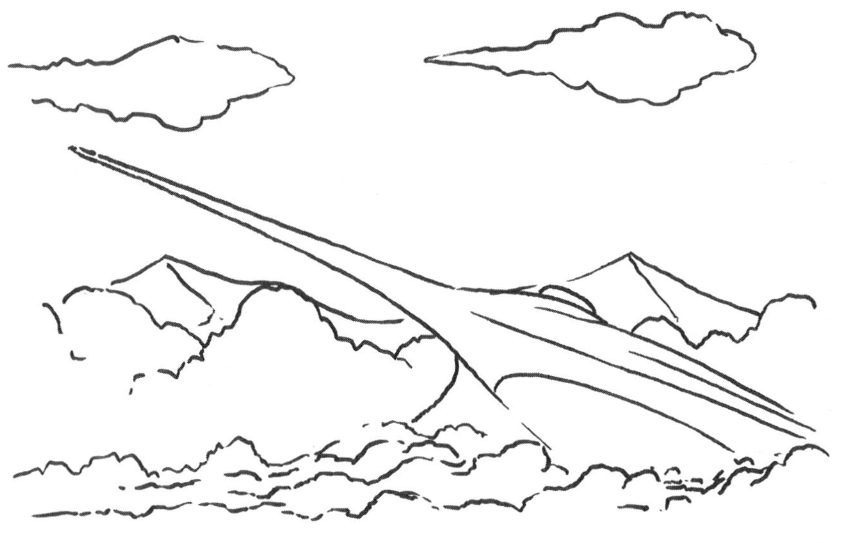

Sinimak looked up at Nojo with pleading eyes. "I meant you no harm, Nojo, " he said with a whimper. "We can still do business," he offered. "I know things, important things, things no one else knows."

"The only thing a slimy bugger like you knows is Lieutenant Zyperion is going to be very angry with you when he gets out of that pit," countered Nojo.

Then Nojo paused to listen for few seconds. The sounds of battle in the rest of the fort had ended. The main sound now was one of Sinimak's soldiers being herded out the gate. "I suspect you'll get a chance to see Zyperion's full wrath in a few moments," he added.

The mere thought of Lieutenant Zyperion made Sinimak panic. "It's here!" he finally blurted out.

"What is here?" quizzed Nojo. "And don't even think about trying to trick us with little crumbs," he cautioned. "Spill all the beans, or I'll toss you into the pit with Zyperion myself."

"The Pillar of Knowledge! The Pillar of Knowledge!" Sinimak squealed in a panic. "It's there in the Fortress of Light. That is why I came to this pathetic planet in the first place."

Nojo nodded, his transparent eyelids blinking rapidly. "Keep talking," Nojo said quietly.

"I didn't even need the vault under Bandilar's castle," explained Sinimak. "I already knew the prize was in the Fortress of Light. I just needed to get into it." Then a sly look crossed his face. "We could be partners, Nojo," he offered again. "I'm sure you have a key, and I know secrets about the Fortress." Sinimak tried to puff himself up as best he could and said, "You need me."

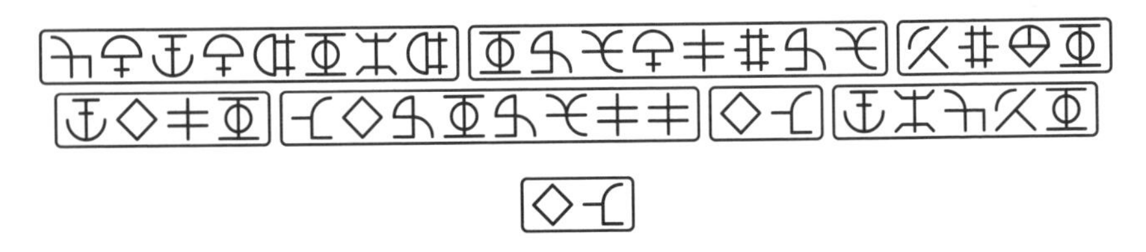

30 Sinimak, the Prisoner

"And what are these secrets?" asked Nojo, skeptically.

"You can't expect me to tell you everything now, Nojo. It's much too complicated anyway," said Sinimak with a slippery smile.

Scott was listening intently and spoke up, "I wouldn't trust him to count to ten without trying to trick us. I say let the Lieutenant have him."

"Ten?" added Jake, "more like five."

"He is a weasel, that is a fact," agreed Nojo. "But if it's true about the Pillar of Knowledge being in the Fortress, then he might be useful. Of course we'd have to keep him on a short leash."

It was then that the fabled Lieutenant Zyperion showed up. The Centaurs had just released him from Sinimak's prison. He looked like a large version of Nojo, but with a bulldog's neck and personality. He was frothing mad. "Where is that slime bag!" he demanded.

Jake had never seen anyone as mad as Zyperion. The Orion glared at Sinimak with such ferocity that Jake thought Zyperion's eyes would leap out of his head and attack all on their own.

Sinimak was so scared that he hid behind Nojo. "Protect me!" he squealed.

Nojo raised his palm in a motion to stop. "Lieutenant, I believe the pile of spittle cowering behind me can help us find the Pillar of Knowledge. Would you be so kind as to let me keep him for a few hours?"

Zyperion stared at Sinimak for a long moment. A large vein in his bald head throbbed explosively as he thought. "Two hours," Zyperion said with finality. "Bring him to the starship in exactly two hours. We may have it flight ready by then." With that, Zyperion turned abruptly and stormed out.

Tondir and Kefreti were coming in at the same time and nearly bumped into the fuming Lieutenant. When Kefreti saw the brothers she cried out, "Jake, Scott, I'm so glad you are all right!"

"Are you kidding? Easy as pie," replied Scott.

"We are pleased to see you are well, Nojo," said Tondir, smiling at the little Orion.

"Thanks to all of you," Nojo responded with a slight bow. "You have my eternal gratitude. Then he added, "And I could use your help again to make sure that Sinimak doesn't escape when he leads us to the Fortress of Light."

Tondir gave Sinimak a sharp look and declared, "The Dark Wizard will give you no trouble while I am around."

"Tally-ho then. We've only got two hours, so let's get moving," said Nojo. "Sinimak, you can tell us how to get into the Fortress of Light on the way there."

As they all filed out of the room, Sinimak sneered at Nojo. "It's easy if you have the key."

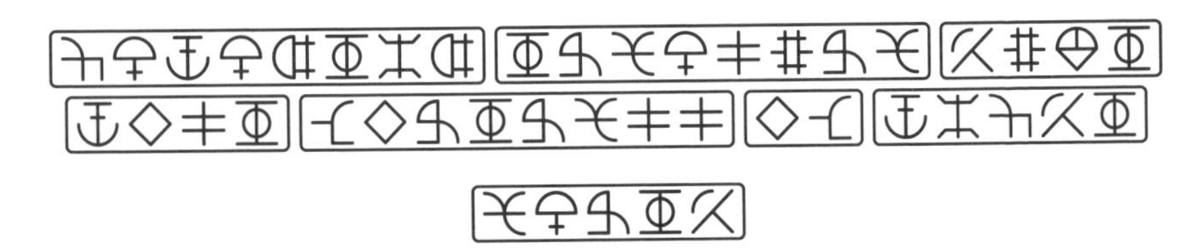

31 The Fortress of Light

It wasn't far from Sinimak's fort to the valley that held the Fortress. As they broke out of the forest, Jake gazed over the alien landscape and marveled at what he saw. It was as Tondir described it, a huge four-sided pyramid stood in the center of a barren valley. A low wall surrounded the pyramid like a fence. Each side of the wall had a gate. In many ways it looked like a pyramid on Earth. The main difference was this pyramid had a beam of perfect green light shooting straight out of the top. Jake looked up along the beam to see where it went, but it simply kept going up and up. It went as far as he could see.

"It looks a lot like that pyramid we escaped from in Egypt, huh?" said Scott.

"You're right," replied Jake. "I bet this one has an entrance for the key keepers too."

"Key keepers, what are the key keepers?" quizzed Sinimak, overhearing the boys.

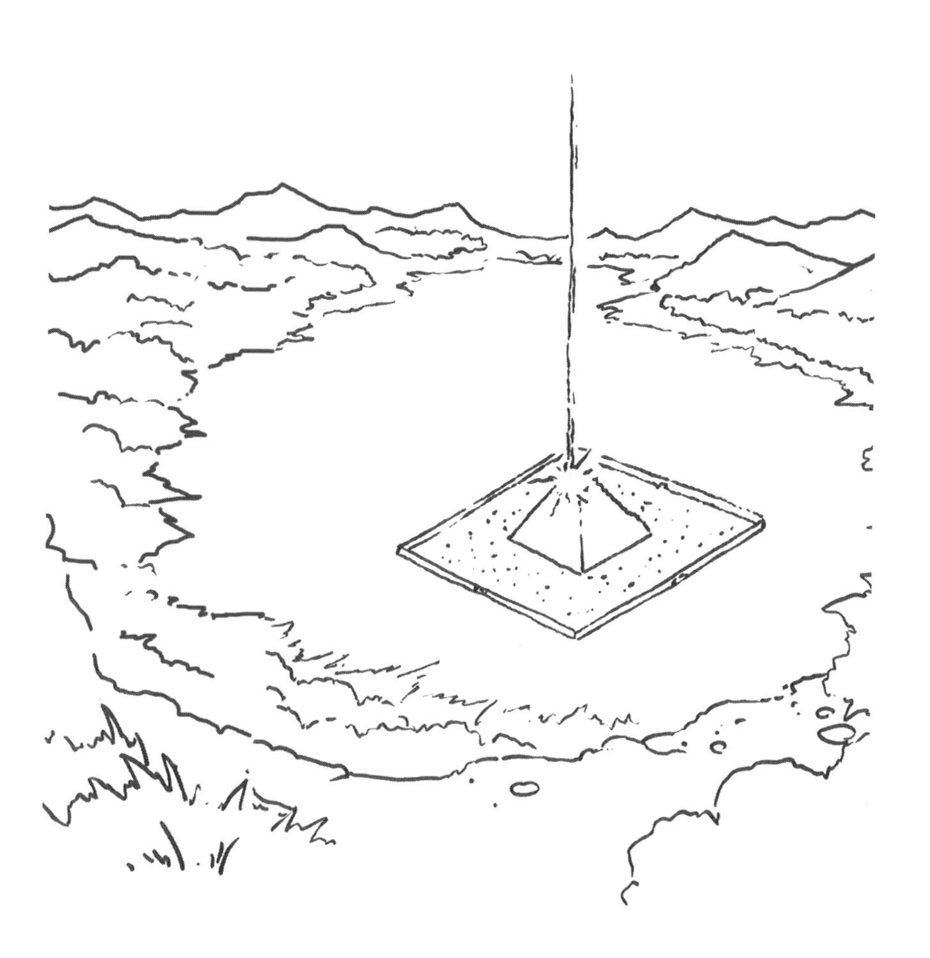

"Don't worry about the key, Sinimak," replied Nojo quickly. "You just tell us where the entrance is and how to get in without harm."

"Not so fast," said Sinimak in an oily voice. "We need to negotiate terms before I reveal secrets it took me years to learn."

Tondir was standing next to Sinimak. He drew two of his swords and held the blades so that they just touched Sinimak's neck. "Negotiations are over, Wizard. Talk," he said calmly.

Sinimak instantly changed his tune. "There, there!" he cried frantically, pointing toward the gate in the right hand face of the pyramid. "There is a spot next to that gate that looks like it might open a secret entrance."

"Then, tally-ho," said Nojo brightly. "We're good at secret entrances."

As they walked toward the pyramid, Scott started to get a strange feeling, like something was just not right. He couldn't put his finger on it at first. Finally, he realized that it was the emptiness. Not a single blade of grass grew in the valley, nor did a single insect buzz in the air. Even the sounds of their footsteps were muffled. Stranger still, there was not a breath of wind, but the air itself seemed alive. It crackled with a mysterious energy that shimmered before his eyes. "This place is very weird," he said to Jake and Kefreti walking next to him.

"Weird? Creepy is more like it," agreed Jake.

Kefreti pointed to the gateway. "And it is about to get even creepier."

Scott looked and saw an open archway in the outer wall. It was a big opening, ten times bigger than a normal door. There was no gate blocking it. At first glance it looked like he could just walk right in, no big deal. As he looked closer he saw that just inside the gate were bones, lots of bones. "Spooky," announced Scott, trying not to get spooked himself. "Weird and creepy works, but I think spooky is the best word for this place. We'll have to remember to come back next Halloween."

Jake had to laugh. "Just be sure and bring your werewolf costume, bud. That would even scare the manxwraiths."

When they got close to the gate, Sinimak blurted out, "There it is!" He pointed to a familiar looking bowl shaped hole in the wall just to the left of the gateway. "I told you I was valuable. Now, where is the key?"

"Key coming through," said Jake as he and Scott stepped toward the Delphian keyhole.

"Where?" asked Sinimak, with a confused look.

Nojo said nothing. He just smiled slowly.

Scott raised a finger as he walked to the keyhole. "The key is right here, Mr. Dark Wizard. It's in our fingers. We're the key keepers, dude."

With no further hesitation Jake said, "Three, two, one, touch." And they did.

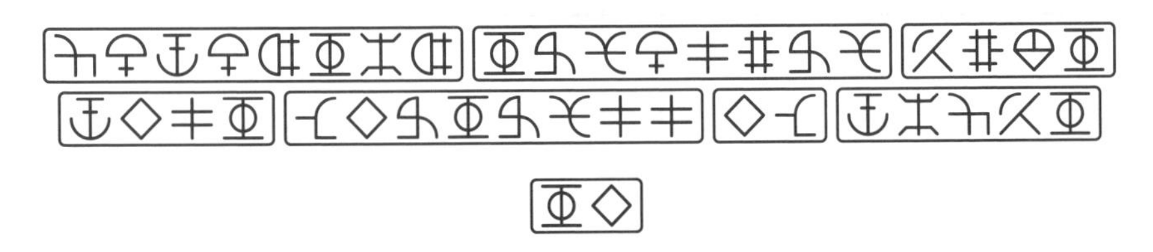

32 The Fortress Beckons

As always, strange Delphian symbols, alien images, and fleeting thoughts passed through the brothers' heads when they touched the center knob of the keyhole. When it was over, they stood back and waited for something to happen. No one spoke a word. They waited but nothing happened. No door opened, no bells chimed, no butler appeared, nothing.

Finally, Scott joked, "Maybe no one's home. Let's just trick-or-treat the next house."

Jake was about to add his own snappy comeback when an idea struck him, "Scott, you're a genius. Maybe they're home and we just didn't see them open the door. Let's ring the bell again. This time focus on all the stuff that passes through our heads."

Scott held his finger next to the center knob. "It's worth a shot," he said.

Jake counted down, and they touched again. Jake focused hard on all the alien thoughts that flashed through his mind. It was the same confusing jumble of symbols, images, and thoughts as the last time. But one word kept forming in his head, "Welcome." He said it out loud.

"Yeah," agreed Scott. "I had exactly the same thought. It's not like I heard the word 'welcome,' but I felt it."

"I think the door is open," announced Jake. "I think we can just walk right through this gate, no problem."

When Jake and Scott started to walk toward the open gate, Nojo called out, "Stop! I can't let you walk through that gate. You may be right, but if anyone is going to walk through that gate, it will be me." He locked his eyes with the boys to make sure they understood. "I'm the one who got you into all this. I'm not about to let you walk into a gate that has killed everyone that's entered it since the dawn of time without testing it first."

Always thinking, Jake countered with his own idea, "Nojo, we know the gate welcomed us. But maybe it only welcomed us. If we are not the one's who step through the gate, it might decide to kill you. How about we all go together? That way the gate knows you're with us."

Nojo thought about that for a moment, then nodded his head and chuckled. "Why does this always happen? Whenever I try to make you safe, you come up with a good reason to walk into danger. Your poor parents, how do they sleep at night?"

"Our parents think we make all this up, Nojo," said Scott with a grin as he started walking again toward the gate. "They think we're out playing in the meadow."

Sinimak took a step back. "This is all very sweet, Nojo," he said snidely. "But I think I'll stay behind and guard the rear."

"I think not," Tondir replied, grabbing Sinimak with both his right hands and holding a sword against Sinimak's side with his upper left hand. "You're with me, weasel. We walk together."

They all joined up into a single row with Scott, Jake, and Nojo, in the middle. Kefreti was on the left and Tondir with Sinimak was on the right. Kefreti commented to Scott as she stepped over a skeleton, "It sort of reminds me of the crypt under the castle back home, only without the spiders."

"You're right. It does look like the crypt," Scott replied quietly. He almost said, it reminded him of a crypt a little too much. But he kept that thought to himself.

And a crypt it was. There were lots bones scattered everywhere. They appeared to be the bones of warriors, treasure hunters, and adventurers of every kind you could imagine. There were many Alserian warriors in full battle gear. Their bones were crumbling, but their shields and swords looked brand new.

Jake was both fascinated and alarmed as he walked through the gate. He figured there would be Alserian bones, but what was more intriguing were the bones of the other treasure seekers. The bones were clearly alien to Alsera. They were the remains of space travelers like themselves. There were various dead creatures in sophisticated battle gear armed with advanced weapons and synthetic clothing. There were even dead aliens wearing full spacesuits with closed helmets.

The fact that advanced aliens had died trying to enter this place struck Jake as a bad sign. Maybe even a very, very bad sign. As he stepped carefully among the many skeletons, Jake was starting to suspect some deadly trap would spring at any second. And then it did.

33 Enter

A brilliant flash of green light erupted from the arch of the gateway just behind them. The light touched the ground in a continuous sheet of luminance and sealed the gate as if it were not simply light, but a solid object. At that same moment there was an extremely loud thunder clap and a shockwave rushed out from the closing gate. The blast pressure from the shockwave knocked all of them to the ground as if they'd been slapped by a giant hand.

Scott was sprawled in the dirt, his ears ringing. He blinked and saw the rotting skull of an ancient treasure hunter lying inches from his face. Scott pushed himself off the ground and onto his knees, then shook his head to clear it. The power of the light that sealed the gate was so intense that Scott could barely look at its reflection in the soil, much less gaze at the light itself. The pure green curtain of laser light had touched down just a few feet behind them. Even from that distance its heat was burning his back. If they hadn't all walked through at the same time some of them would be dead now.

Jake didn't know if another laser blast was about to obliterate them or not. Whatever was going to happen, he figured the smart move was to move. He scrambled up from the pile of bones he'd been tossed into and looked toward the pyramid. There in the side of the pyramid was an open doorway. It hadn't been there a second before, of that he was sure. "A door!" he yelled to the others. "Get to the door!"

Scott needed no invitation. He jumped up and then joined Jake, who was pulling Kefreti out from under an ancient shield. "Come on!" he urged, helping her up and pushing her toward the door.

Nojo got up. He saw that Jake and Scott were okay and turned to make sure Tondir wasn't hurt. He could see Tondir standing over Sinimak, who was cowering on the ground. Sinimak was burying his face in his hands and shaking like a leaf. "We can't leave the Dark Wizard, Tondir," cautioned Nojo. "He might get into mischief."

Tondir nodded and then picked up Sinimak with his lower hands like he was a sack of potatoes. "Come with me you whimpering dog," he said.

As they all ran the few yards to the doorway, Jake kept thinking some other trap was about to be sprung. But this time he was wrong. They made it to the doorway without so much as a flea jumping out at them.

"See, easy as pie," said Scott between panting breaths. "We told you the keyhole said welcome."

Nojo shielded his eyes and glanced back at the wall of light blocking the gate. He nodded slowly. "By Jove, I believe you are right. That laser wall was not meant to kill us. It was meant to seal the Fortress once the key keepers entered." Then he looked at Jake, "Jake, I owe you my life. If we hadn't done as you suggested, I'd be toast about now."

Jake just smiled. "No problem, Nojo. Like you said, this is a dangerous place."

"Speaking of danger," replied Nojo, "what other dangers await us inside, Sinimak? Tell us everything you know right now, or you go no further."

"Valuable information should be rewarded," Sinimak replied in a weaselly voice. Then he saw Tondir start to draw one of his swords and abruptly changed his tune. "All right!!" he squealed, pulling away from Tondir. "There is an inscription on the opposite side of the outer wall. It translates as 'THE FOUR GUARDIANS MUST AGREE YOU ARE THE ONE, BEFORE THE SEEKER MAY DRINK FROM THE SUN.' That's it, I swear," he insisted. "That's all I know. I have no idea what it means."

Nojo looked Sinimak square in the eyes for a few moments before announcing. "I believe him." Then he added with a bit of caution in his voice, "Tally-ho, shall we?"

Nojo led the way. He held Sinimak's gravity wand in front of him and light beamed out of it like a flashlight. The corridor was made from some kind of black material that seamed to suck up Nojo's light. That made it difficult to see where they were going, but they went on anyway, cautiously moving forward into the dark.

After a few short minutes they saw a point of light in front of them. As they continued on, the light grew and they could see it was really many lights, all moving in a slow dance. Finally, they emerged from the corridor into a vast cavern. They all stopped. No one said a word. They simply stared, jaws dropping, astounded by what they saw.

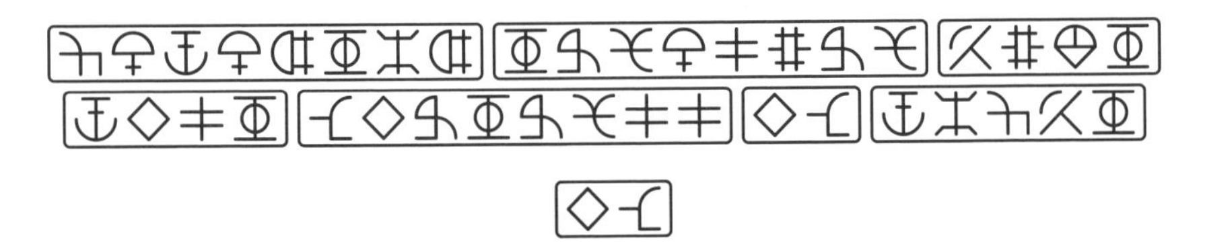

34 The Planetarium

Jake was the first to break the silence. "It's like a giant planetarium," he observed, while gazing upwards at the suns, planets, and moons all orbiting each other in the colossal room before them.

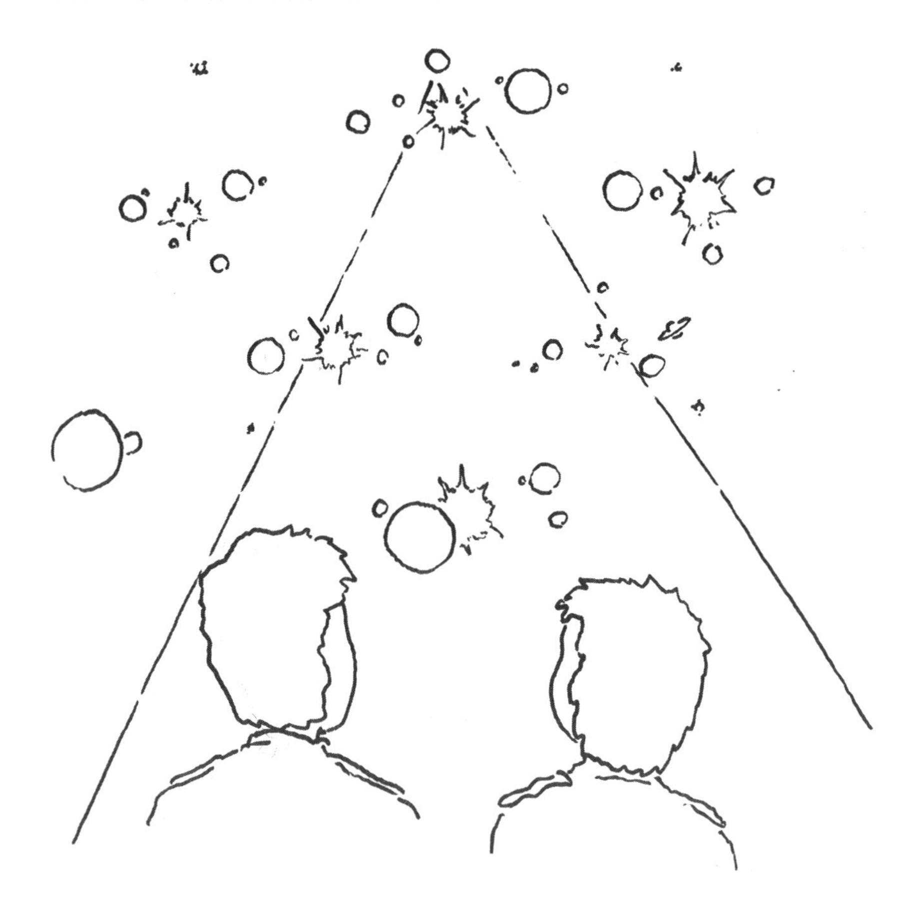

"It reminds me of the waypoints. Like we're inside a waypoint," Scott added, as he took in the scene. The room was the size of a large football stadium with four walls spaced far apart. It had a jet black floor and the ceiling came to a point high above them. Within it Scott counted six small suns. One sun near the bottom, four in the middle, and one near the top. Each sun was orbited by several planets, though each planet was not much larger than a house. Some of the planets even had moons. Each of these mini celestial objects was unbelievably detailed. Clouds swirled in the atmosphere of the planets. There were tiny snow covered mountains, forests, and oceans. They didn't look like models at all. That prompted Scott to ask, "Are they real?"

Nojo waved the wand about the room and took some readings. A puzzled look crossed his face as he announced, "I'm not sure. Their gravitational pull is far greater than their size would create. They appear to be miniature versions of real suns and planets, but I can't imagine how that could be." Nojo turned to Sinimak, "Do you know anything about this?"

But Sinimak did not appear to hear Nojo's question. He was fixated on something else. In the center of the floor was a four-sided pillar about twenty feet tall. In such a massive room it seemed rather small. On each of its faces Delphian symbols continuously flashed and scrolled. Stationed around the pillar was a ring of seats with control panels in front of them.

Sinimak stared with wild eyes at the pillar. "I knew it," he muttered to himself. "It is here!" Then he giggled with glee, "At last, the Pillar of Knowledge is mine!"

"It's not yours, Sinimak," Nojo countered. "If you're lucky, the Hyper-Marshalls will take your assistance into consideration when you're sentenced for your crimes."

Sinimak turned toward Nojo, a scowl on his face. "No!" he screamed. "It's mine! Mine!" With those words he ran towards the Pillar of Knowledge.

"Stop!" cried Tondir, starting to chase after Sinimak.

Before Tondir got more than a single step, Nojo grabbed one of Tondir's lower arms. "Wait! It isn't safe!" he shouted. "The wand readings! There's no gravity in there!"

Perhaps Sinimak didn't hear Nojo or chose to ignore him. Either way, the result was the same. He ran only a few yards before crossing a thin glowing line in the floor. When his foot left the smooth black surface on his very next stride, it didn't propel him forward toward the pillar, it sent him up. Sinimak went up into the blackness, up into the swirling planets, up toward the ceiling far, far, above.

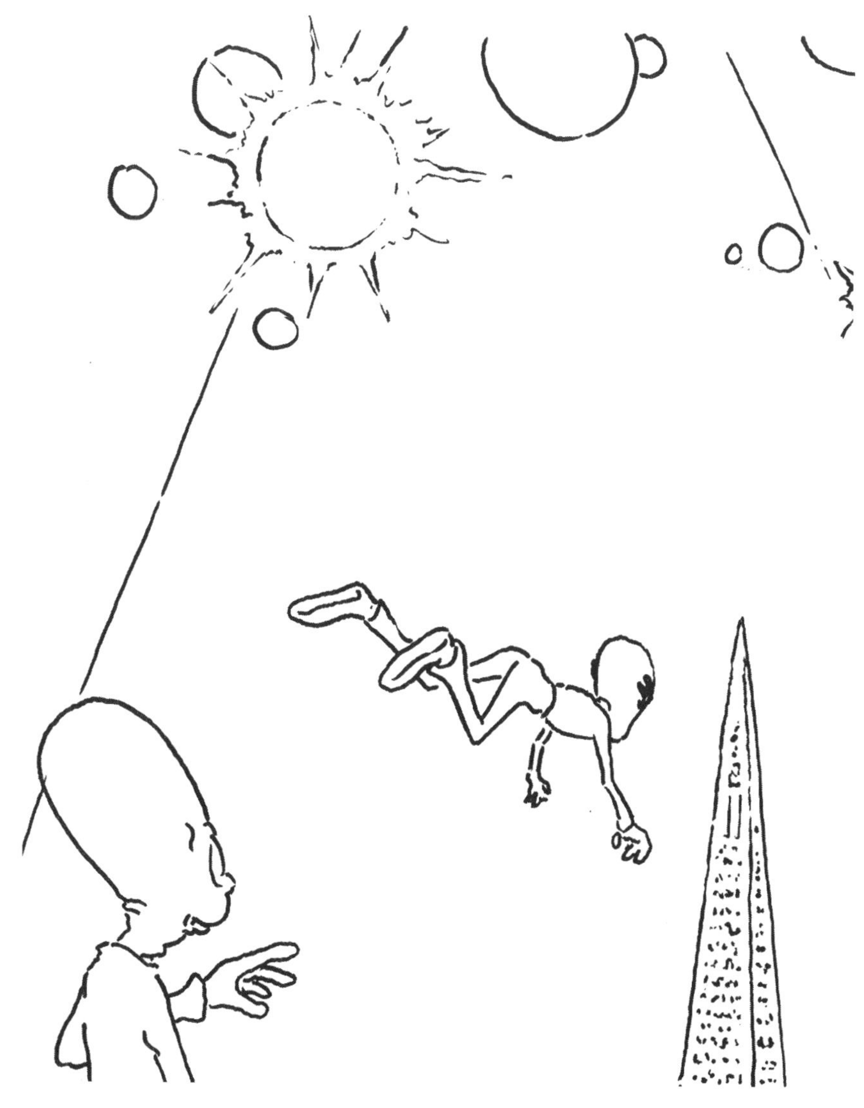

"Help!" screeched Sinimak, when he realized what was happening. "Nojo, save me!"

Nojo made some quick adjustments to the gravity wand and pointed it at Sinimak. "Hold on!" he shouted to Sinimak, who appeared to be drifting ever faster upward. "I'll try and pull you back."

Sinimak's upward travel slowed, it looked like it was working. Sinimak smiled with relief until he saw that one of the orbiting planets was about to pass near him. He felt himself pulled towards it. "More gravity, you fool!" Sinimak screamed at Nojo.

"I'm using full power now!" Nojo yelled back.

As the house-sized planet got closer, Sinimak was pulled even faster towards it. He screamed, "No!"

Even with Nojo trying to counter the planet's gravity, the planet pulled Sinimak into its orbit. Sinimak flailed his arms and legs, but that had no effect. Sinimak's path through the planetarium was altered again a few moments later when a passing moon's gravity flung him upward yet again. "Do something, you idiot! Do something!" Sinimak wailed. He was getting further and further away. His shouting grew fainter and more distant with each passing moment and each new pull from one of the many tiny planets.

Nojo kept the wand pointed at Sinimak, but after a while it had almost no effect. "There is nothing more I can do," Nojo muttered to himself.

Jake watched Sinimak as he was pulled from one planet to the next. Each time he drifted further upward. It was as though the most powerful gravitational field was at the very top. This seemed odd to Jake because the top of the pyramid appeared to be empty. Then he looked closely and saw something, something small and black. It wasn't just black, it was blacker than black. Jake thought he knew what it was. Sinimak was being pulled into a black hole.

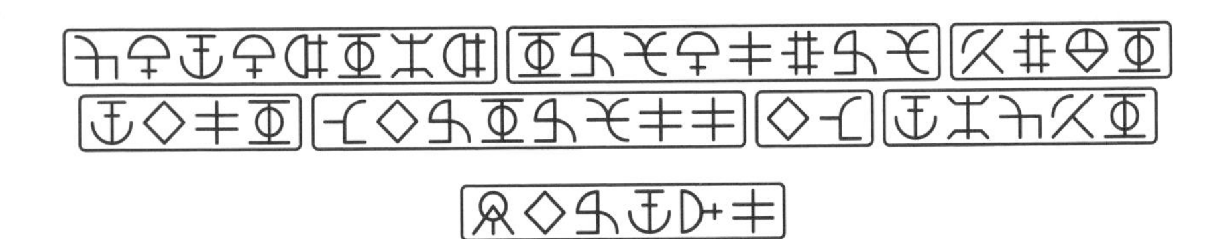

35 Gravity

The gravity of the black hole at the top of the pyramid was relentless. It pulled Sinimak inward in a spiral pattern. Sort of like going down a drain, only it pulled Sinimak up. His shouts grew fainter and fainter. After a few minutes Sinimak was far above them. They could see him approach the nearly invisible black hole. At the very last moment his body stretched out toward the small black hole, as if he was made of Silly Putty. He became as tall as a giraffe and as thin as a pencil just before he disappeared.

For several moments no one said a word. It was Scott who spoke up first, "I thought I'd seen some freaky stuff on this planet, but I was wrong. Watching Sinimak get sucked into a black hole is the freakiest thing I've ever seen."

"Good riddance," Kefreti said. "He would have stolen the universe if he could."

"We should thank him, actually," Nojo replied. "We are now very well aware of the dangers here in this chamber of planets and suns. Clearly, we can't simply stroll over to the Pillar of Knowledge. But there must be some way to get there. This is just one more test the Delphians have set for the key keepers.

"I think you're on to something, Nojo," said Jake. "I'll bet it has something to do with what Sinimak said had been carved into the outer wall." Then Jake recalled Sinimak's words, "THE FOUR GUARDIANS MUST AGREE YOU ARE THE ONE, BEFORE THE SEEKER MAY DRINK FROM THE SUN."

"But which sun? What are the four guardians?" asked Tondir. "There are six suns and many planets. Are some of them the four guardians? Or are any of them the guardians?"

"Does one of the suns have four planets?" asked Kefreti, trying to understand what Tondir was saying. "Maybe a sun with four planets is what we need to drink from. But, how do you drink from a sun?"

"You can't drink from a sun," replied Jake with certainty. "That must not be what they mean. They must mean you get something from one of these suns. But I don't know which one."

Nojo examined each of the little solar systems in the planetarium before announcing. "None of these suns has exactly four planets. So, there must be some other answer."

Scott had been silently looking around this amazing planetarium. He too was stumped by the puzzle. He tried counting planets, suns, and even moons, but the puzzle didn't seem to add up. Finally, when he stopped looking at all the whirling objects, it all became clear. "We're in a pyramid," he said simply. Then he added, "That is the answer."

"The answer to what?" quizzed Tondir.

"To the riddle," said Scott. "A pyramid has four sides. The four sides are the guardians."

Nojo pulled his gaze from the many planets and suns and looked at Scott. "Good observation, lad. Four sides, four guardians, that adds up," Nojo agreed. "But where are these guardians?"

Scott smiled and winked at both Nojo and Jake. Then he pointed almost straight up. "I think that is a guardian."

Jake looked where Scott pointed. He saw a floating silver ball. It was high along the wall of the pyramid above them. It was much smaller than the planets. It was even smaller than the smallest moons in the planetarium. It was almost invisible in the blackness. The one thing that made it noticeable was that, unlike every other orb they could see, it didn't move.

"There!" shouted Kefreti, pointing to a nearly invisible silver ball half way up on the left wall of the pyramid. "There is another one."

"And there as well," added Tondir, pointing to a ball along the right wall.

"Dude, you're a genius," was all Jake said.

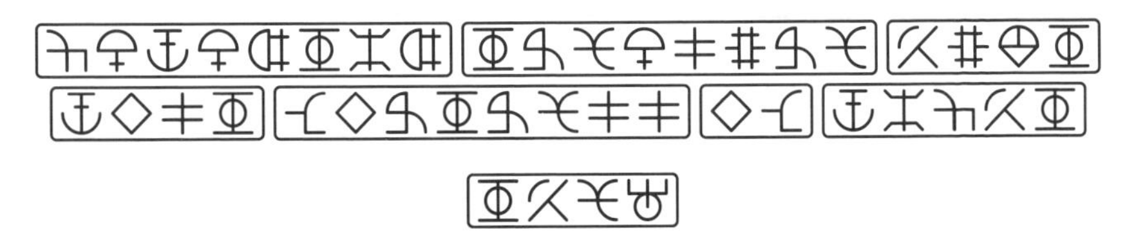

36 The Guardians

"They look like the knobs Scott and I touch for the keyholes," Jake observed. "I bet all we have to do is touch all four of them. Then we'll get to drink from the sun, whatever that means."

"I think you're right," replied Nojo gazing across the planetarium. He was looking for the fourth ball, but it was too small to see across the giant cavern. "The fourth one must be on the far side. We'll find it when we get there. Now we just have to figure out HOW to get there."

"It would be easy as moolish pie if we could fly," said Scott.

Jake excitedly nodded his head. "Scott, you've done it again, we'll fly! Sinimak flew, so we can fly too."

Nojo looked at Jake, "Are you crazy? You saw what happened to Sinimak. You'll be bounced around like a ping pong ball and then get sucked into a black hole." He shook his head. "I'm not letting that happen. We'll simply leave and come back with the right equipment.

Lieutenant Zyperion will have full gravity control flight packs on his ship."

Jake and Scott exchanged looks, and Scott glanced toward the entrance they had come in. "Aren't you forgetting something, Nojo?" asked Scott.

Nojo's transparent eyelids blinked a few times. "Like what?" he inquired.

"Like the giant laser beam gate that closed behind us," said Scott with a grin. "We can't get out. So Jake and I have got to touch those little balls. It's the only way."

Nojo slowly blinked one more time before muttering, "If your father knew what I know, he would change your name from the monkey boys to the danger boys." Then he said firmly, "I see your point, but if you're going to fly, then I will go with you. We'll use my gravity wand to pull us toward planets we want to orbit. Let's hope it works."

Tondir stepped forward, pulling the two sword scabbards off his back. "Here," he offered. "Use the belts from my scabbards to tie yourselves together. That way you can't get separated."

"I'll help tie you," insisted Kefreti. "I learned some very strong knots from the deckhands on the ship."

Kefreti used Tondir's belts to tie all three of them together at the waist. Nojo was in the middle, Jake was on the right and Scott was on the left. "There," if that doesn't hold you, nothing will."

Nojo waved his wand around the room and then pointed at the red line in the floor just in front of them. "That line in the floor is where the gravity ends," he said. "Once we cross that line it will be like we're floating in outer space. The only difference is we'll be able to breathe."

"No problem," insisted Scott. "Nojo will use his wand to grab passing planets and moons. We just swing from one planet to the next until we get there."

"It's as good a plan as any," agreed Nojo. "Now, I suggest we start with one foot on the gravity side of the red line and one foot on the no-gravity side of the red line. That way we can get a good push toward that first ball."

They walked up to the red line together. Scott put his right foot across it. Then he started to sing and do a little dance, "You put your right foot in. You pull your right foot out..."

Jake joined him and they sang together, "…You do the hokey-pokey, and you shake it all about…"

Nojo couldn't help but chuckle. "You two are truly crazy," he said with a smile. "All right, danger boys, let's fly."

"We aim straight for the ball on three," said Jake, looking up towards the ball. The ball was about midway up the side of the pyramid, well inside the no-gravity area. "Three, two, one, jump!" he shouted. And they did.

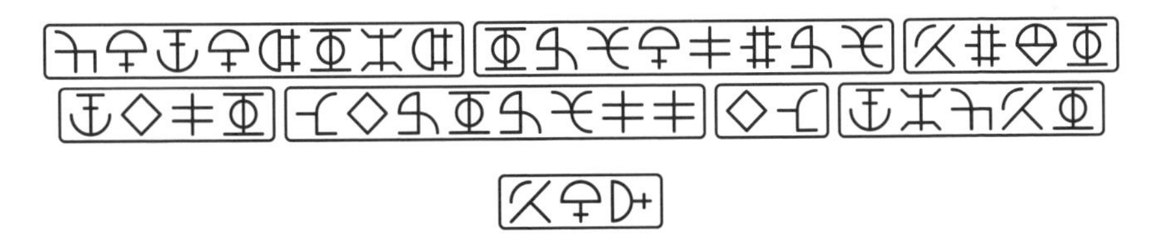

37 Gravity Assist

The three of them flew like arrows through the weightless room. Their arms were stretched out in front of them like they were in the legion of superheroes. It was incredible.

"Scott, has anyone ever told you that you look just like Superman," kidded Jake as they flew.

"Not even close," Scott replied. "I'm Danger Dude, defender of small kitty cats. You can be Super Dude," he suggested.

"Danger Dude and Super Dude need to grab onto my belt, now!" commanded Nojo. "The gravity of the planet on the left is pulling us off course. I'll use my gravity wand to pull us back towards the guardian ball."

The boys grabbed Nojo's belt and they flew on toward the guardian ball. It looked like a minivan sized beach ball. It had about a dozen short spikes sticking out of it. The spikes weren't pointy; they looked more like antennas of some kind.

"Grab onto those antenna things!" Scott shouted.

They were flying up pretty fast, and Nojo called out, "Grab quick!" They all hit with a thump and frantically grabbed antennas, even as Nojo apologized. "Sorry about that," he said. "The gravity in this place is all bonkers. It's hard to tell how much gravitational pull you have on something."

"Are you kidding? That was awesome!" hooted Scott. "Let's do it again!"

"Let's get this one to 'AGREE WE ARE THE ONE' first," suggested Jake.

"There," said Nojo, pointing to a small golden knob set into a round hollow on the face of the giant silver ball. "It's a keyhole, just like the others."

Unlike everything else in the planetarium, the guardian balls seemed to have no gravity of their own. So Scott spun himself around in zero gravity to hover over the keyhole. "The usual then," he said

"Three, two, one, touch," chanted Jake. Delphian thoughts passed through his head as usual. When the ball started to glow with a deep green light he knew their plan was working.

"We are the one. Yeah, baby! We are the one," Scott started to sing. As he sang, he noticed that the suns in the planetarium grew brighter and the planets seemed to move faster. "Cool," he thought to himself.

"Fine job," declared Nojo. "Now, we fly on to the next guardian. That one there, on the right" he said, pointing.

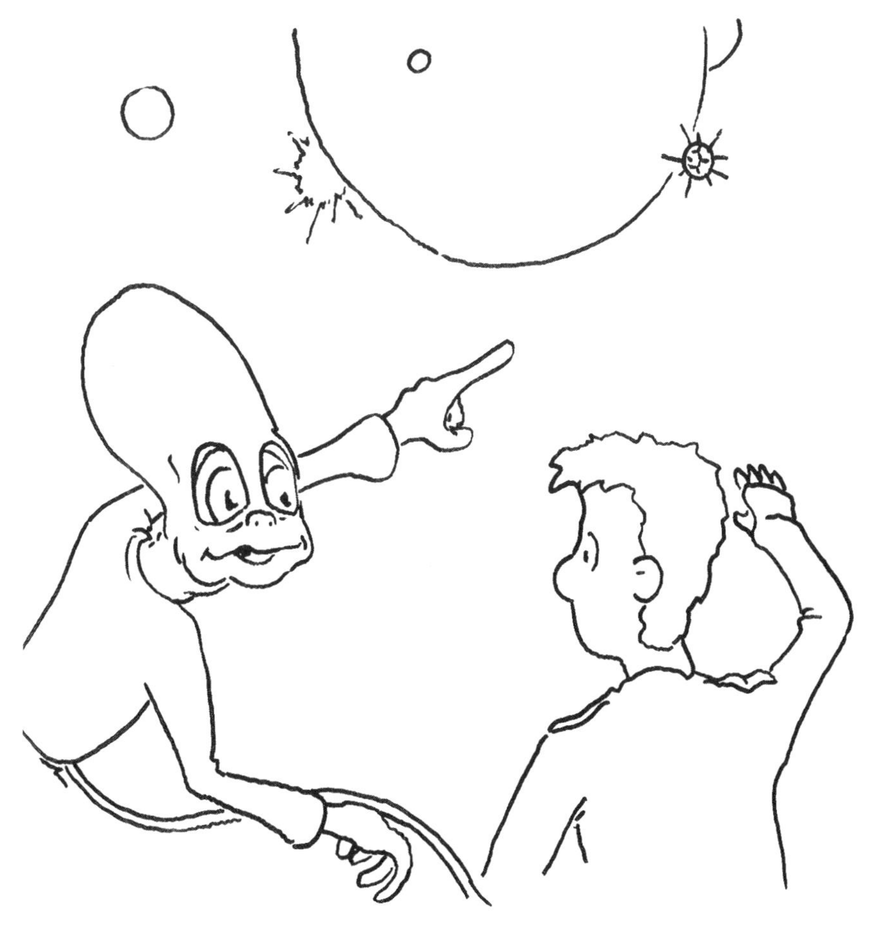

Jake saw the guardian ball Nojo pointed to was in the middle of the pyramid wall. It was at the same level as this first one and about a soccer field away. The only snag was a small sun and its planets between them and the next guardian ball. “Those planets are blocking our way,” Jake observed.

“Right you are, Jake,” said Nojo. “We’ll have to hitch a ride on one of the outer planets by using the wand. So hang onto my belt when we leap.”

Scott clung to the guardian ball for a few minutes watching the planets orbiting their sun. He looked for one that would carry them in the right direction. “There,” he said finally, pointing to a swirling gas planet that looked a bit like Jupiter. “That one looks like it’ll swing close to the next guardian.”

“Good eyes, Scott,” agreed Nojo. “Launch on my three count. Leap at the planet just after it passes us. Its gravity should pull us around the corner.”

“Got it,” both boys responded.

“Three, two, one, go!” Nojo barked.

It worked just as they planned. They were pulled along by the big planet’s gravity. When they got to the right spot in the orbit, Nojo switched the focus of his gravity wand from the planet to the second guardian ball. The ride behind the planet had them moving pretty fast, but they managed to grab on to the second guardian just as before. They found the keyhole and turned on that guardian as well. Now the second guardian glowed green, just like the first.

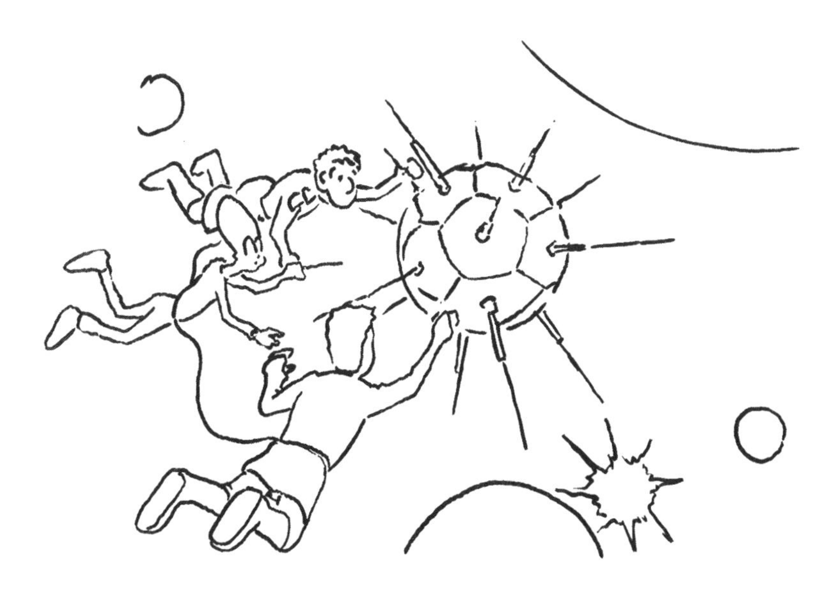

As they prepared to hop to the next guardian, Scott noticed the six suns burned ever brighter and the planets moved even faster. "Everything is speeding up," he announced.

Nojo eyed the zipping planets and nodded his head, "I believe you are right. This next jump will be harder."

38 The Planet Dance

Jake eyed a blue planet with puffy clouds, vast oceans, and chunks of green land dotting its surface. It was beautiful and reminded him of Earth. The arc of its orbit would bring them close to the third guardian ball. "There!" he shouted, pointing at it. "The Earth-like planet will swing us around the corner."

Nojo looked quickly. Planets were now orbiting rapidly and he only had a moment to decide. "Right. She'll do. Ready, steady, now!"

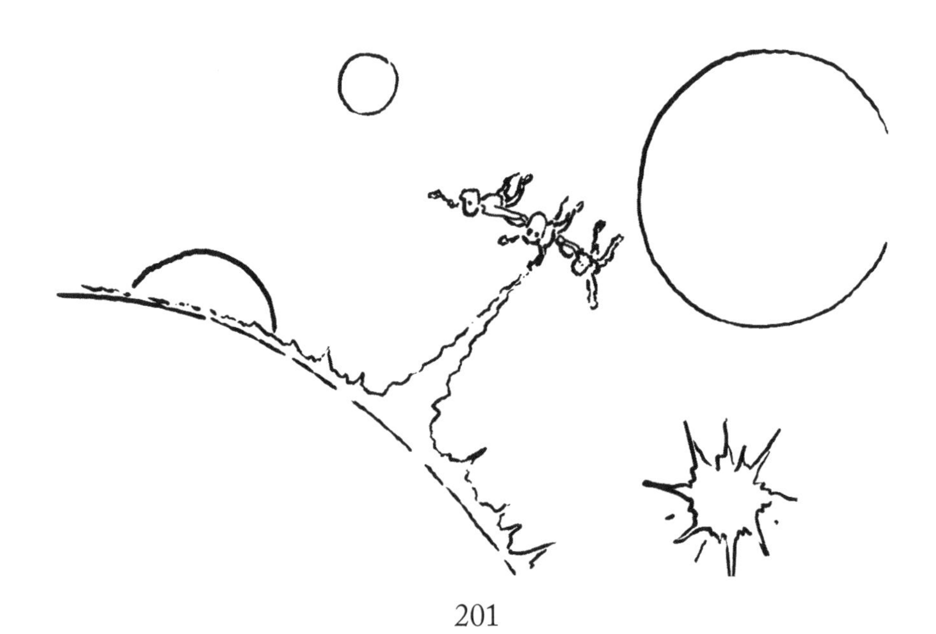

They all leapt toward the blue planet just after it whizzed past them. Nojo had his arms outstretched, both hands holding his gravity wand. Jake and Scott each held on to Nojo's belt with one hand and were being towed by Nojo. The gravity of the blue planet pulled them all along. They had become moons.

It was a faster ride this time than last. Not only was everything moving faster, but Jake felt a strong gravity pull from the planet. It felt far greater than the last planet, even though this one was a bit smaller. The planet's pull accelerated them rapidly. This super hero stuff was a thrill. "Yeehaa!" Jake whooped.

"Yea-hooo!" Scott echoed back as they whizzed around the corner of the pyramid and headed toward the third guardian ball.

Nojo switched the wand's focus from the blue planet to the guardian ball. The trick had worked twice before, but this time they were moving faster. The wand was pulling them close, but it looked like their trajectory was a bit off. They were going to pass just to the left of the ball. "I do believe I've fumbled it," Nojo observed calmly. "We're going to miss."

"Not if I can help it," Jake said with determination. Timing would be everything. Just before they sped past the guardian ball, he let go of Nojo's belt. At the same instant he pushed himself away from Nojo, toward the ball. He stretched his right hand out as far as he could and just managed to grab an antenna. He was almost pulled off when the tether linking him to Nojo and Scott went tight, but somehow he managed to hold on.

"Way to go, Super Dude!" cheered Scott, as he swung into the ball and grabbed hold. "We should change your super hero name to Captain Stretch."

"Well done, lad. Well done," congratulated Nojo as Jake and Scott touched the keyhole. The third guardian turned green, just like the others. Then things started getting really interesting.

Scott floated next to the antenna he was holding and stared at all the planets and moons. They were going bonkers. The suns burned fiercely and the planets were accelerating to more than twice the speed of this last jump. The orbits of the planets were starting to go crazy. They no longer spun in nice little circles. They traced long curving arcs and passed dangerously close to one another. Some of the smaller moons even broke free of their planets and flew across the planetarium. One of the free moons collided with a sun and was swallowed in a giant fire ball. "Wow! I'm glad that wasn't us," was all Scott could say.

"Not a fate I would be wishing for either," agreed Nojo. "We're going to have to be sharp on this next jump. No room for error."

"I've got a good one," cried Scott. "That big red gas planet at nine-o'clock!" He pointed to his left.

There was no time to make an analysis of the red planet's orbit. Nojo simply shouted, "Go, go, go!"

The boys grabbed Nojo's belt and they leapt after the swirling red orb of gas. It was a wild ride, and at first it looked like a good choice. It felt like they'd just snagged a car zipping past on the freeway, but at least it was taking them in the right direction. Then Jake saw something ahead of them. It was a loose moon on a collision orbit. "Nojo, look out for that moon!" he screamed.

Nojo saw it just in time. A small yellow moon was almost dead ahead and aimed straight for them. At the speed the moon was moving it would be like getting hit with a freight train. He quickly switched the focus of the gravity wand and aimed straight toward the fourth guardian ball. The timing was wrong, but he had no choice. "Hold on!" he yelled.

Scott saw the quick change in their orbit did the trick. The moon just missed them on the left. His eyes were now glued on the fourth guardian. It was coming up fast, and it was not looking good. Nojo's wand was pulling hard toward the ball, but they were going to pass on the outside. "I've got this one!" he called as he let go of Nojo's belt.

Scott pushed off from Nojo. He stretched out as far as he could for an antenna. He reached the end of his tether well before they passed the ball. It was no good. He could see they were going to miss by a few lousy feet. He couldn't reach it. He struggled against the tether to get a hair closer, but to no use. His heart stopped for a beat. With all these planets going crazy, they would almost surely be killed before they got another chance to reach the fourth guardian. "No! No!" he thought. Suddenly he recalled his father telling him once, "You can do anything if you set your mind to it."

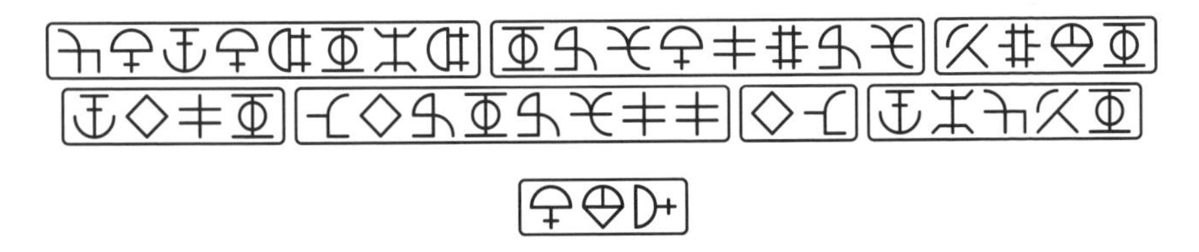

39 Yo-Yo

Exactly how he thought of it, Scott will never know. It just popped into his head. In a flash he reached into his pocket and pulled out a yo-yo. It was the yo-yo Kefreti had given him back on the sailing ship. Those quiet times of playing on the ship seemed so long ago now, almost a lifetime ago.

Scott stuck his finger through the loop and swung the yo-yo end around his head like a lasso. He would only have one chance, so it better be good. As they whizzed past the guardian ball, Scott let fly the yo-yo. It wrapped around one of the antennas and pulled tight.

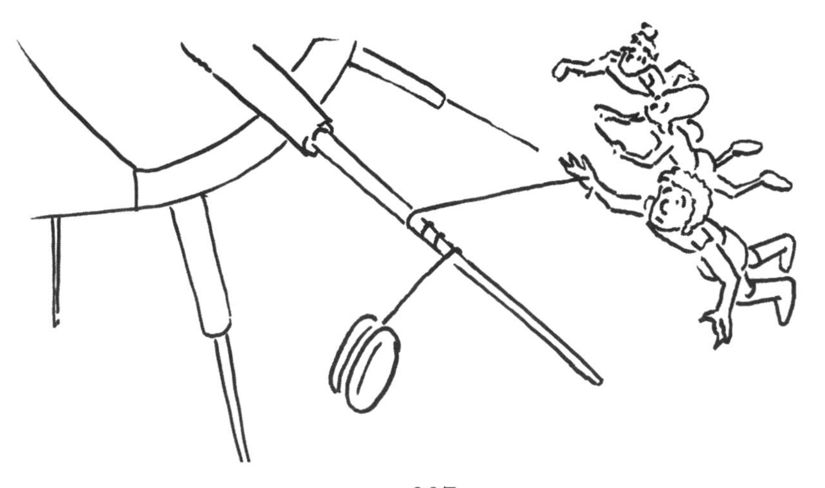

"Yow!" Scott howled, when their weight yanked on the yo-yo's string. If the string weren't made of tough leather, it probably would have broken. As it was, it felt to Scott as if his finger was being pulled off. But it worked. He'd lassoed the ball and they all swung in to grab an antenna.

"Danger Dude! That was awesome!" hollered Jake. "I thought we were black hole chow for sure."

"Definitely a pickle," said Nojo with his eyes wide. Then he repeated himself. "Definitely a pickle. We owe you our lives."

Before Scott could even say, "You're welcome", two moons collided. The collision was way too close and extremely loud. Bits of moon were flying in all directions. A giant chunk was headed straight for them. Scott and Jake didn't even bother doing their usual count down. They just looked at each other, nodded quickly, and touched the keyhole on the last guardian ball.

The ball glowed green like the other three. Then something new happened. Brilliant green laser beams shot out of the top of each of the guardian balls. The beams all converged at the very top of the pyramid, where the light vanished into the black hole.

Jake looked up. "The black hole!" he shouted. "It's growing!"

Scott would have looked but his eyes were glued on the chunk of moon speeding toward them like a bullet train. He was trying to decide if they should jump or not. Then he saw the fragment of moon unexpectedly swerve upward. "It's going to miss!" he announced excitedly.

As they watched from the guardian ball, the stars, moons, and planets started rising. Everything except the guardian balls was moving toward the black hole at the very top of the pyramid. The black hole started sucking them all up in a spectacular light show. The green lasers converging on the black hole seemed to corral everything. The crazy orbits and high-speed race of the planets was done. Everything spiraled up in a surprisingly calm and orderly procession. Each planet, star, and moon, took its turn to be gobbled up by the black hole. With each new thing it ate, the black hole grew a tiny bit. Finally, the very last planet was gone. No sooner had it vanished when a beam of laser light shot out of the black hole and down into the top of the pillar at the base of the pyramid.

"I love it when a plan comes together," joked Jake.

"That was the plan?" kidded Scott back. "You planned for us to almost get smashed to bits and sucked into a black hole?"

"I do believe the key word in the plan was ALMOST," said Nojo, joining in. Then he pointed at the ground. "Now we just need to get down. Hang onto me," he instructed. "I'll use the gravity wand to set us down gently."

As they came down with the help of the gravity wand, they could feel the normal gravity of Alsera returning to the pyramid. Nojo saw Tondir and Kefreti standing at the edge of the giant cavern. "Gravity has returned," he called out to them. "You should be able to walk out here now."

Kefreti came running out and hugged Jake and Scott. "We saw the whole thing! I was so worried about you. I don't know how you survived this crazy place. You will be legends on Alsera for all eternity."

The brothers blushed. "It was no big deal. Yeah, anybody could have done it," they mumbled.

"I don't think just anyone could have turned that on," said Tondir, pointing at the Pillar of Knowledge in the center of the room.

As if to highlight Tondir's words, the Pillar started to warble, chirp and hum. It seemed the Pillar was singing a Delphian welcoming song.

40 Pillar of Knowledge

The shaft of green laser light from the black hole entered the Pillar of Knowledge at its apex. Jake could feel the heat from the powerful laser before he even got close to the Pillar. It should have burned the Pillar to a crisp, but instead the laser seemed to bring it to life. The multiple screens and control consoles around the base of the Pillar were now frantic with symbols, lights and sounds. Jake couldn't make any sense out of it. At times the symbols and sounds seemed familiar, sometimes totally alien. It was almost random chaos.

"What is it doing?" Scott asked.

"I have no idea," replied Jake. "Maybe it is like a computer, starting up after thousands of years of being asleep."

"I believe you are right, Jake," added Nojo. He was pointing his gravity control wand alternately at the Pillar and the black hole above them. "It appears the black hole is both the power source and the data storage device for the Pillar of Knowledge. It looks like this pillar in front of us is simply the computer screen. The Fortress of Light itself is really the Pillar of Knowledge."

Scott raised his hand, as if he was at school. "Hold on there, Nojo," he said. "I thought black holes were called black holes, because nothing can leave them, not even light."

"True," replied Nojo. "Yet, there it is. The Delphians were masters at controlling the fifth dimension and beyond. I suspect this black hole is a portal, much like a wormhole into other dimensions we cannot see."

"Maybe the Pillar of Knowledge itself will tell us," injected Jake. He walked up to a control consol on one side of the Pillar and stared at the symbols. "Nojo, do you know how to work this?" he asked hopefully.

Before Nojo could reply, Scott piped up. "Hey, Pillar of Knowledge!" he yelled at the Pillar. "Yo, what's up, Pillar Dude? So, how do you work anyway?" It was just Scott being goofy. He was certainly not expecting what happened next.

The random noises and screen messages on the Pillar monitors stopped immediately. They were replaced by an image of Earth on all the screens. A clear and soothing voice seemed to surround them. It said, "Welcome, Jake and Scott, voyagers from Earth. You have proven yourselves worthy of great knowledge and with it great power. The guardians have determined that you are The One."

Jake was too stunned to speak for a second. How did it know their names? Finally, he regained his voice, "The guardians were those balls we touched, right?"

"The balls were simply locks," the voice responded. "The guardians have been watching you ever since you touched the first keyhole on Earth's Moon. If you had not been The One, the guardians would have changed the codes. You could have never gotten here."

Jake was still confused. "Excuse me, Mr. Pillar, or Sir, or whatever your name is, but I don't get it. Why are we The Ones? We're just a couple of kids."

Scott could almost hear a chuckle in the Delphian voice when it replied. "The guardians know your very thoughts. You are The One because you did not come here for yourselves. You did not come in conquest or for power. You came for each other and your friends, you came for adventure, and you came for the good

of the universe. The guardians would only give great power to those who would use it well."

Scott started to smile. He turned to Jake, "Jake, this is awesome! It's like we have our own personal genie. I know what I want."

Jake glanced at Scott and shook his head. "It's not like that. We have to give the Pillar of Knowledge to all the peaceful planets in the universe."

"I know, I know," agreed Scott, "but we haven't eaten in, like, forever! Maybe the guardians can pull some strings for us." Then he turned to the Pillar and spoke very politely, "Mr. Pillar Dude, this may seem like a strange question, but is there a snack bar around here?"

41 Home At Last

Nojo took the controls of their spaceship as the craft entered Earth's orbit. "Good piloting boys," he complimented while he vectored the ship through the atmosphere toward the meadow.

It was hard to believe they were home. They'd only been gone a week, but what an amazing week! They'd had tons of adventures, fought many battles, and found the Pillar of Knowledge. After they turned on the Pillar of Knowledge they were able to turn off the laser gate and let in Lieutenant Zyperion. The Orions were already storing the knowledge from the Pillar for all peaceful planets, including Earth. The Orions had even talked to the President of the United States. Soon, the whole world would know about Jake and Scott's adventures.

Fortunately, getting back from the Fortress of Light was a lot easier than getting there. The Lieutenant's men had fixed their starship, so the trip back to Nojo's craft had only taken a few minutes. After saying goodbye to Kefreti and Tondir they blasted off for Earth.

Jake had just finished changing into his regular clothes when Nojo's ship streaked into a daylight landing. Jake knew their parents wouldn't be worried. He recalled from their last trip to the Lost Universe that whenever you return from another universe you always return at the same time you left. So, as far as their parents were concerned, they'd gone into the woods only moments ago.

As the boarding ramp lowered, Nojo called to the boys, "Don't forget, boys. I'll be picking you up tomorrow for a visit to the White House." Then he put on his parent voice and added, "Wear good clothes. You'll be meeting the President, and you want to look your best."

"Yes, Nojo," replied Scott as he ran down the ramp. "We promise."

"And tell your parents they're invited too!" Nojo called out.

"Okay, we will," shouted Jake as he followed Scott into the woods. "See you tomorrow!"

Scott was the first one to reach the backyard. His mom was outside watering the flowers. "Mom, Mom!" Scott yelled. Then he ran up and gave her a big hug.

"Hey, little buddy," their mom said, hugging Scott back. "I love my hugs, but what is this for?"

Jake came running up and hugged his mom too. "We missed you. We haven't seen you for a whole week." Before she could even say anything he added, "It just doesn't seem that way to you because we went to the Lost Universe again."

"You went to the Lost Universe?" said their mom with pretend surprise. "And here I thought the Lost Universe was, you know… lost."

"Mom!" groaned Scott. "I know you don't believe us, but it was insane. We had to fight surf dragons and manxwraiths!" he exclaimed, while dancing about the yard pretending to sword fight. "Then we got to ride the centaurs and I did a triple back flip. Have you ever seen anyone do a triple back flip on a centaur?" he asked intently.

His mother didn't bat an eye. "A double maybe, but never a triple. That might be a centaur flipping world record," she replied earnestly.

Scott barely noticed his mother's response. "Then we thought we were going to get sucked into a black hole in this giant planetarium, but we didn't because I was the Danger Dude and Jake was the Super Dude, but we changed his name to Captain Stretch." Then Scott took a big breath and added as a complete afterthought, "Oh, and we're going to see the President."

"Sounds like a very action-packed morning to me," said Mom with a firm nod.

Jake rolled his eyes. "Mom, I know you think we make up all these stories, but they're true," he said with as serious a face as he could manage. "We really are going to meet the President of the United States tomorrow. You and Dad are invited too."

"You boys are such a hoot," Mom said laughing. "I'm always amazed by..." But then she suddenly stopped. Her eyes went wide and fixed on something in the forest behind their house. Her mouth dropped open. She was speechless.

Jake turned and saw Nojo's ship rise slowly above the trees and float towards them. "That's our friend Nojo, Mom," he explained.

The ship drifted silently over the yard. The boarding ramp came down while the craft was still a dozen feet in the air. Nojo stood near the edge of the ramp.

Nojo waved a friendly hello and smiled at their mom. "Good afternoon. You must be Jake and Scott's mom. I'm Nojo," he said in his charming English voice. "I'm sure you're very proud of your boys. I know I am."

Mom couldn't manage any real words. She just nodded and slowly murmured, "Uh-yeah."

"Don't forget, I'll pick you up right at eight o'clock. We don't want to be late for the President," Nojo said with a smile. He waved again, the boarding ramp closed, and the ship vanished in a blink.

Their mom stared at the spot where the ship vanished for a long moment. Finally, she turned to Jake and Scott. "Boys," she said, "your father is never going to believe this."

Real or Fiction

Drinking from the Sun – Could a Black-Hole Shoot a Laser Beam?

Scott was correct when he said that light can not escape a black hole, which is why they are called black holes. However, there is a theory that black holes can act as a portal into other dimensions and possibly other universes. So, it is not entirely out of the question that some advanced technology could use a black hole to store lots of information in a very small space. Black holes could be the ultimate memory storage device. They are so dense, that if you could use them to store data they could hold all the information on the internet in something smaller than a speck of dust.

Are There Really Other Universes?

The short answer is no one knows. However, it is very possible, and maybe even probable, that there are other universes and we simply can't see them. Our own universe began about 13.7 billion years ago in what is called the big bang.

There are a handful of plausible theories as to what started the big bang, but most of them involve other dimensions besides the ones we are familiar with. In our everyday lives we deal with objects in three dimensions (1.up-down, 2. left-right, 3. forward-backward) and a fourth dimension of time (things change with time, so it is considered a dimension). However, there is no clear physics or mathematical reason for those four dimensions to be the only ones. As far as modern physics is concerned it is equally plausible that there are five or more dimensions. We simply can't see the other dimensions.

Amazingly there is actual evidence that other dimensions do exist. Some known properties of atoms can only be satisfactorily explained with the existence of additional dimensions. The birth of our own universe is also difficult to explain without the existence of other dimensions. So, if our own universe was most probably born from some unknown event in some unseen dimension, then it is equally probable that other universes are also born in this same way.

If we went to another universe could you really move super quick and swim through solid objects?

Again, no one knows, but it is possible that the laws of physics would be different in another universe. Some physics theories, like sting theory for instance, speculate that each universe is made from very tiny strings that vibrate in dimensions we can't see. The vibration of these strings governs the basic behavior of atoms. In some universes the string vibration would be so different than ours that planets and people could not even exist because gravity and other forces might be too strong or too weak. If we visited a universe that that was made from strings that vibrated close to the speed of our own universe then we might be able to go there, but there could be weird effects.

In our story we speculated that Jake and Scott's atoms vibrated a bit faster than atoms on Alsera. That would make everything Jake and Scott did seem very fast to Alserans. It might also allow them to "swim" through apparently solid objects, much like radio waves of different frequencies move through the air without interfering with each other.

Could There be Such Things as Centaurs and Manxwraiths?

Why not? There are probably billions or even trillions of planets in the many universes that have advanced life. On our imaginary planet of Alsera all advanced creatures have six limbs. There's nothing in evolutionary theory that says creatures must have two arms and two legs and look like us. Centaurs and manxwraiths would be plausible evolutions of six legged creatures.

Is There Really a Pillar of Knowledge?

Our current internet is already a Pillar of Knowledge far beyond anything that could have been imagined even a hundred years ago. Today's ordinary computer hooked to the internet can answer almost any question you've got, tell you the weather half way across the world, and show you live pictures around the planet. If an internet connected computer could be sent back in time, ancient man would have thought it was magic that could only belong to the gods.

Very possibly there is an intergalactic internet with an intergalactic-wikipedia and search engine. This intergalactic internet would be something like the Pillar of Knowledge. Maybe one day we'll make contact with an alien civilization that can give us access to that intergalactic internet. Now THAT would be something worth surfing.

Are There Such Things as Gravity Wands?

There aren't any gravity wands on Earth just yet, but I predict that they will exist here someday. The truth is, we're not exactly sure what gravity is or how it is transmitted. There are theories about gravity waves and gravity particles called Gravitons. However, to date no one has ever been able to detect either a gravity wave or a Graviton. So, maybe the existing theories are wrong. Some current experiments in gravity modification indicate that it may be possible to alter local gravity. Maybe you can be the person who invents the gravity wand. I know I'd buy one.

Secret Message

There's a decoder at the end of each Galactic Treasure Hunt book that decodes the Delphian words at the start of each chapter. To find out what happened to Jake and Scott when they met the President, decode the alien word at the top of each chapter in order.

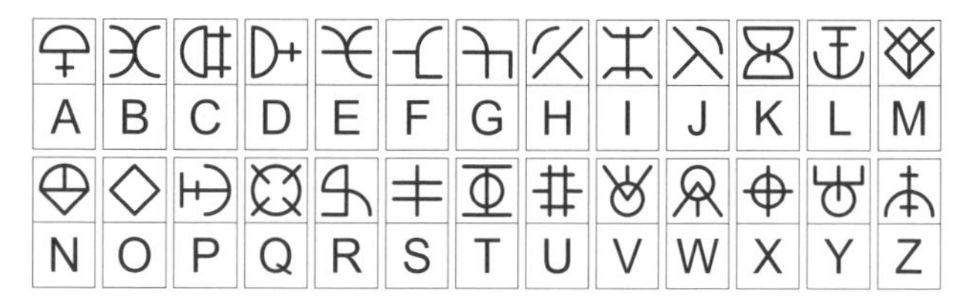

Jake and Scott send you
Greetings!
From the White House Lawn.

A note from the Author

I loved writing the Galactic Treasure Hunt series. I hope you enjoy reading them as much as I enjoyed writing them. This series came about because I was having lunch one day with my buddy Chris (the illustrator). At the time, we both had children about five or six years old. We both read bed time chapter books to our children. We were complaining about how boring some of them were. So, we decided right then and there to write and illustrate a book of our own. At the time we didn't know if it would actually get published, but we figured we'd do it anyway.

Chris and I talk about what happens in each story over lunch. Chris is very good about pointing out things that couldn't work that way, or that don't make sense. That helps me keep the stories at least remotely plausible, in a science fiction sort of way.

The characters of Jake and Scott are based upon my own two boys, Finn and Hatcher. Their difference in age and the basic personalities of Jake and Scott are pretty much the same as Finn and Hatcher's. The character of Nojo, is sort of based on me, though I'm not entirely bald. If I had a starship, I'd certainly want to go exploring in it.

Be sure to check out these other exciting titles in the Galactic Treasure Hunt series!